I0739286

The Conceit of Memory

BIFF DUNNIGAN

Phrase Bound Publications
Woodland, California, USA

http://www.phrasebound.com

Publisher's Cataloging-in-Publication Data

Names: Dunnigan, Biff, author.
Title: The conceit of memory / Biff Dunnigan ; edited by Bert MacKenzie ; cover design by Leona Craig.
Description: First edition. | Woodland, California : Phrase Bound Publications, 2015.
Identifiers: LCCN 2015942444 | ISBN 978-0-9963075-0-5 (paperback) ; ISBN 978-0-9963075-1-2 (EPUB) ; ISBN 978-0-9963075-2-9 (Kindle) ; ISBN 978-0-9963075-3-6 (audiobook).
Subjects: LCSH: Fiction--Psychological aspects. | Family secrets–Fiction. | Detective and mystery fiction. | BISAC: FIC025000 (FICTION / Psychological) ; FIC031080 (FICTION / Thrillers / Psychological).
Classification: LCC PS3604.U554 C66 2015 | DDC 813/.6–dc23.

First Edition 2015
3 5 7 9 10 8 6 4

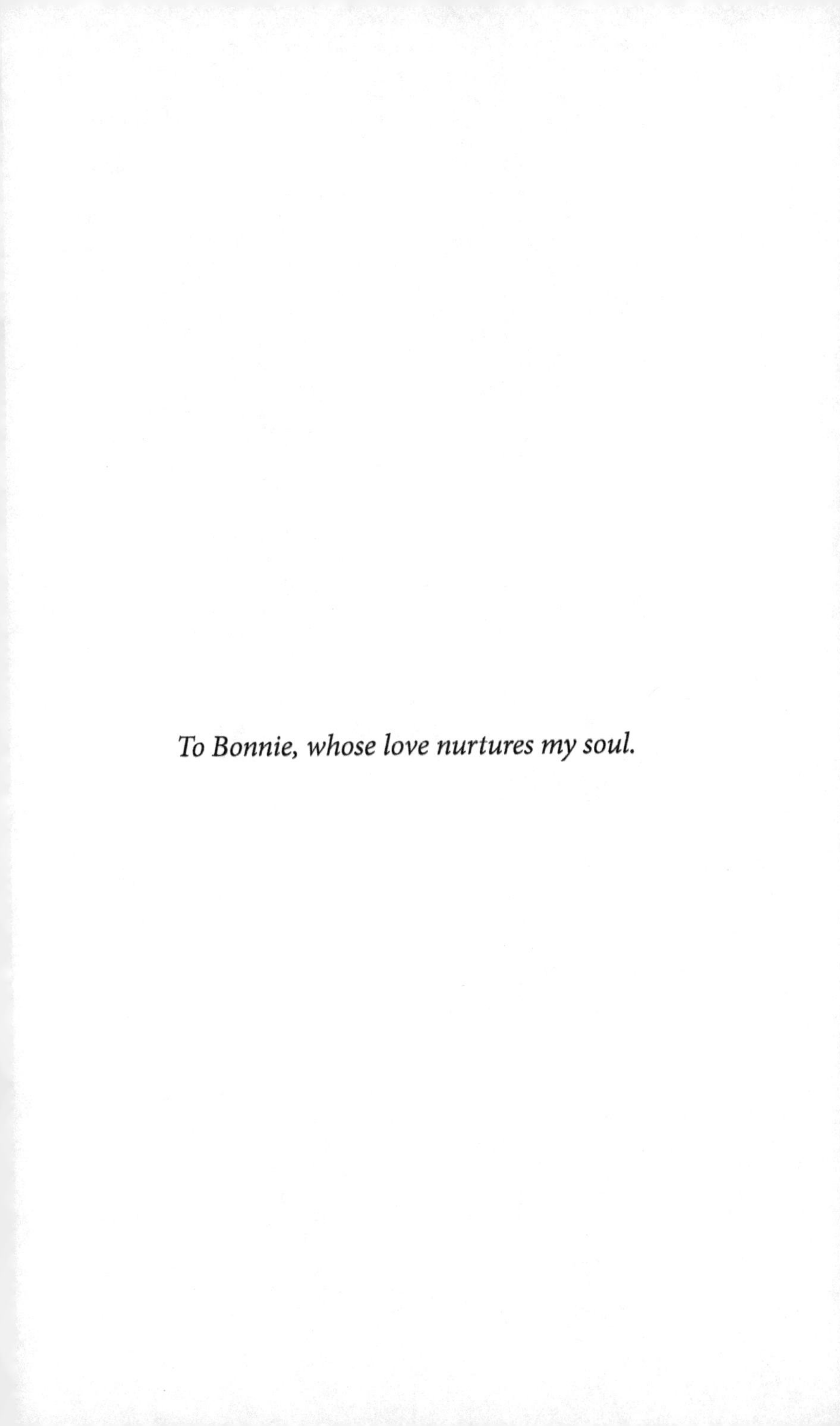

To Bonnie, whose love nurtures my soul.

Contents

1

Embarrassing myself at the church

The absolute best a man will ever look in his life is how he happens to look wearing a tuxedo on his wedding day. I had no doubt this adage was true, as I paraded myself in front of a full-length mirror on what would prove to be a most fateful day. Tall and trim, I was indeed looking better than any man had a legal right to look. *Had I made the correct choice, however, I pondered, having selected the all-white tuxedo rather than the traditional black one?* More specifically, was it better to resemble a slender polar bear or a svelte emperor penguin? What really mattered was that my beloved fiancée, Bianca, had approved of the choice, and nothing more stood in the way of her becoming Mrs. Trevor Crawford by sunset that day. Nothing could go wrong—or so I thought.

My best friend in the world, my cousin Matt Wilkins, was to be my best man. I had a few age-appropriate co-workers whom I viewed as both friends and peers; any of them would have seemed likely candidates to stand up for me at my wedding, but in my heart, I knew that there could have been no other choice than Matt to fulfill the role. The duty fell on him to make sure everything was in order and that everything went off without a hitch, at least until I myself was "hitched." The bright sunlight of a warm summer day illuminated the musty room.

Matt stood by, gazing intently at my reflection in the mirror. "Leave the last button of the vest unfastened," he said, in an apparent effort to be helpful.

"I know, I know," I replied.

Even if his parents hadn't accepted me as a foster child nearly twenty-five years ago, Matt would forever be like a little brother to me. I knew deep down I would always protect him, although on that particular day, the roles were reversed: He had assumed responsibility to look after me, and if need be, come to my rescue.

A gentle rap at the door interrupted our moment. "They're ready, sir," said the disembodied voice of one of the church assistants on the other side of the door.

"So am I" was my confident reply. "Let's go, Matty," I said, as I exited the room, with Matt following closely behind. Despite my elated anticipation of the day's festivities, my agitated excitement surfaced through the pores of my skin in the form of an unwelcome nervousness and stilted trepidation. I kept reminding myself of the day's goal: not just a happily married life, but a lifetime to spend with my beloved Bianca. Keeping that goal firmly in mind helped to calm me, at least momentarily.

The narrow hallway into which we walked was dark and unadorned. It gave little indication that it led directly to the inside of an expansive church, almost cathedral-like in its immensity, with its brightly colored stained-glass windows filtering the afternoon sunlight and adding a rainbow-tinted hue to even the most drab object in sight. As Matt in his black tuxedo, and I in my white, strode from behind the curtained arras onto the ceremonial platform, the enormity of the whole spectacle hit home. A sea of five hundred faces, nearly all of them on the bride's side of the audience, seemed to beam with warm smiles and hushed well-wishing. It made me even more nervous, but in a comforting sort of way.

On my side, in the front, was my foster family— the Wilkins clan—consisting of both of my foster parents, Joe and Angela, and their daughter Emily, all of whom seemed to be flashing encouraging glances at me. My birth mother, whom I had always called Auntie but whose real name was Alma Crawford, was sitting behind them, which at the time, caused me some concern: *Why wouldn't she be sitting up front*, I wondered, *since I, her only child, was to be the star of this show, or at least the leading man?* It wasn't as if my side of the family were footing the bill for the glorious shin-dig; that not-insubstantial burden had fallen on the Dawsons, Bianca's parents, or more specifically, her father.

In fact, I caught a glimpse of Mrs. Dawson, front and center on the bride's side, appearing already to be sobbing into her handkerchief, although the regular pacing of the sobs, coupled with her furtive glances to see if anyone were noticing, made me suspect that hers were merely manufactured tears for the benefit of the crowd. In any event, she was positioned at such a vantage point that she could hardly miss even a moment of her only child's wedding.

Our officiant, Rev. Harrington, had entered from the side of the rectory and was standing on the platform in the center. The stately cadence of a familiar, baroque-period tune drifted through the air to accompany the march of the groomsmen, escorting the bridesmaids as if they were beauty-pageant winners, elegantly parading down the carpeted runway. The groups separated by gender on either side of the platform. The Maid of Honor walked without a partner up the aisle, followed by a cherubic toddler haphazardly strewing petals of roses or some other red flower at irregular intervals from the basket she was clutching. The music faded as the processional came to a dignified end.

The church organ started to crank up the traditional wedding march. A hush came over the audience, and there, at the church entrance, Bianca appeared, with Mr. Dawson at her side to lead her down the aisle. What they say about how good a man looks on his wedding day goes double for a bride. Bianca, the love of my life, looked absolutely radiant as she glided, in measured step with the march, toward me and our future life together. I doubted I had ever seen her more beautiful than on that day and at that moment. Seeing her under these circumstances was both exciting for me, as a man, and humbling that she had chosen me for a life partner. I was utterly unprepared that the elation I felt was about to become one of the most shameful and embarrassing moments of my life.

The closing measures of the march coincided with Bianca's arrival at my side. I had hoped to be the first one to lift her veil; instead, her father did so. The sight of her gorgeous face made my knees buckle ever so slightly, and I could have sworn that the whole room, already dappled with the warmth of sunlight, glowed a little brighter in the aura of her beauty. Her father then kissed her cheek, or at least, that was what it looked like from my vantage point. I started to reach out to offer to share with him a gentlemanly handshake, but by that time, he was already taking his seat next to his wife in the front. As Bianca and I stood together facing forward to the preacher, I felt we were on the verge of being united, not just legally, but spiritually.

I sensed the presence of my cousin flanking me, while the pastor seemed to be waiting for complete silence before beginning to address everyone in attendance. He spoke in a loud, slow, pontificating voice that ensured no word would go unheard, even to the ears of the mice that routinely dwell in the corners of such immense churches. "Dearly Beloved," he intoned, "we are gathered here today in the presence of God to witness and bless the joining together of Bianca and Trevor in Holy Matrimony—"

At that moment, a sense of dread washed over me. I felt like a wave of terror had just swallowed me, pulling me down into the briny depths of an ocean filled with the tears of human sorrow. The sensation I was feeling hit the pit of my stomach like a deliberate punch, and I instantly grew queasy and staggeringly dizzy. It was not a sudden case of "cold feet," that much I knew. Matt was to my left, and I could have simply turned to him, but instead, in my dizzy state, I spun instinctively to my right, so that I found myself facing the crowd.

From my right, I heard Matt ask, through clenched teeth, urgently yet somehow rhetorically, "What in the world are you doing, Trevor?" His mouth agape, he lowered his glance toward the front of my trousers. I saw out of the corner of my left eye a terrible sight. Bianca, her once-beautiful face contorted into a horrified grimace, had similarly fixated her eyes on the same nether region of my body.

I was still reeling with dizziness and nausea, and a kind of numbness enveloped me to the point where I was no longer aware that I was still inhabiting my own body, but I managed to tilt my head forward so I could see what had become the center of everyone's attention. To my everlasting shame, one of the pant legs below the crotch of my trousers was visibly dampened with a large dark-yellow stain, whose color stood out all the more in contrast against the white of my ivory-colored tuxedo. I had, quite inadvertently, peed my pants like an undisciplined little boy.

At first, the audience of onlookers was quiet. Oddly, I hoped someone would laugh or clap or make some other kind of noise to draw attention away from me.

Instead, the ongoing silence reverberated in my ears. This was not, it turned out, something that any sane person would or should find amusing. I had physically recovered my bearings, but I wasn't sure I had figured out what I would attempt to do or to say next.

I saw Mr. Dawson bolt from his seat. With a comforting arm around his daughter's shoulder, he gently led the now-sobbing Bianca to the side, but as he did so, he gave me such a glare that I knew immediately what he was thinking. I could hear his voice in my head, scolding me with "How could you do this to my daughter, you animal? We're a well-to-do, refined family—my brother-in-law is a United States Senator, for Pete's sake—and I always knew I shouldn't have allowed Bianca's infatuation with some low-born, glorified bank teller to get this far. You've ruined her life, not to mention our family's reputation. You'll pay for this, Crawford. Oh, you'll pay dearly." He had told me on numerous occasions that all he ever wanted was for his only child to be happy, and so long as I was the one who could deliver that happiness to her, he had grudgingly accepted me into the family. He was, however, neither prone to nor known for being forgiving, let alone forgetting.

Matt grabbed my arm in a vise-like grip and said, "Dude, we've got to get outta here, like, right now. Let's go. Go!"

Dear, trustworthy Matt: *How like him to have remained clear-headed during such a crisis.* Without hesitation, he ushered me back behind the curtain, through the narrow hallway, and into the dressing room from which I had earlier emerged so confidently less than quarter-of-an-hour earlier. He lifted the duffel bag he had brought precisely to take care of my street clothes; his plan had been to watch Bianca and me drive off as a married couple and then later drop off the bag at my apartment or keep it until I returned from the honeymoon. He was reaching into the bag and tossing my clothes at me, saying, "Better change."

Removing the coat and vest was like escaping a straight-jacket. The jeans, sweatshirt, and sneakers were a much more comfortable outfit than the tight tuxedo with its button-down shirt, form-fitting cummerbund, and now-soiled trousers.

I mulled over and over in my mind how this whole incident could have happened and, given that it had indeed happened, how so unlike me it had been. I fancied myself a man of reason, mostly level-headed. If I had to pick my worst fault, it would be an occasional burst of impatience; I always approached things methodically, some might say ploddingly, but I was known at inopportune moments to act impulsively. Taking short steps, broken up with an unexpected surge of ambition and confidence, was how I made my way in the world. I pondered whether the incident could instead have been a subconscious attempt to extract myself from a commitment I was inwardly unwilling to make. *No, that could not be: I loved Bianca and would never do anything—consciously or unconsciously—to hurt her.* What I needed was some time to think; eventually, I would figure it all out.

We emerged from the back entrance of the church. "My 'whip' is parked on the side," Matt said, gesturing toward the right. "Let's blow this place before they even realize we're gone."

2

How I first met the Dawsons

When Bianca first asked me to meet her father, Mr. Dawson, I was a bit hesitant. He was the patriarch of a wealthy family who oversaw a commercial empire. As a bank loan officer, I'm not the type of person who was even on Mr. Dawson's radar, let alone his idea of a good match for his only daughter.

It was a mild autumn day as Bianca and I drove to the Dawson estate for lunch. I had known from the moment I saw her that I would be proposing to her someday—whether she'd deign to have me was a concern for another time—so I was prepared eventually to have to endure the meet-the-parents ritual. We had been dating for two months and were both serious about a long-term relationship. This luncheon, then, was the natural evolution in taking the next step in our commitment to each other.

Of course, this wasn't some absentee father waiting to meet me: This was a doting parent who treasured every moment with his child and wanted only the best for her. He later confessed to me that, when he looked at Bianca, he didn't see the twenty-eight-year-old woman she'd become; no, he saw the bright-eyed little girl whom he would toss into the air as she giggled every morning he went off to work. He would never see her as she actually was, only as he cared always to remember her.

When I pulled into the driveway of the Dawson home—I would be tempted to call it a mini-mansion—Mr. and Mrs. Dawson were standing on the porch in apparent anticipation. I was sure their eagerness was about seeing their daughter, not to run their skeptical eyes over her latest boyfriend. This was evident when, as Bianca emerged from the passenger side of my car, they gave no notice to me, while they embraced her as if she had survived a storm at sea and had been feared lost forever.

Only after several minutes of what looked like self-adulation did anyone even acknowledge my presence. "There you are, Crawford," Mr. Dawson said, as his glare signaled that he was accustomed to dominating any conversation in which he happened to be engaged, no matter the rank or title of the persons involved.

"Yes, I'm here, ready to meet my future in-laws," I replied. An awkward silence hung thickly in the air, until Mrs. Dawson emitted a gentle, twittering chuckle at my impropriety. "Well," I stammered, "what I mean is, I've never met anyone as wonderful as your daughter, so if I'm going to dream, might as well dream big."

Mr. Dawson had already extended his hand but recoiled slightly at my messy attempt to introduce myself and declare my intentions. He seemed to look at me askance, and I feared I would never fully recover back in his good graces, today or in the years to come. Such telling glances—the kind that express more than words ever could—were, in my experience meeting people on a daily basis in my line of work, a rarity; Mr. Dawson's face, though, was perpetually full of them. It made me wonder how a man, so familiar with the concept of exhibiting his displeasure openly, could successfully navigate a business world often based on subtlety and cunning. Yet, as I stood in the shadow of his enormous house, it was obvious he managed his family matters quite differently than he did his business affairs.

I made a mental note to ask him someday to play poker with me. I marched forward and grasped his reluctant hand. I shook the hand with the hope of shaking off a bad first impression. Of course, this wasn't an employment interview. No, it was much more important than that. An unwise hire could always be fired. A poorly chosen prospective son-in-law should first be subjected to the worst kind of intimidation a father could dole out. It was his duty, yet it was also a role in which Mr. Dawson seemed to relish.

"I'm a big dreamer myself, young man. How else could I have convinced my own bride to take a chance on me?" He turned to Mrs. Dawson and said, "Didn't it work out well for us, Elsa?" Mrs. Dawson smiled with an expression of pure delight and nodded almost imperceptibly but did not speak. I gathered that, between them, Mr. Dawson did most of the talking. Bianca also revealed a knowing smile, as we all walked into the house where I awaited further interrogations from Mr. Dawson, enhanced or otherwise.

The entrance to the Dawson mansion was decidedly impressive. The heights of the ceilings were so imposing that, as we entered the foyer, it was like walking into a cathedral. I didn't recall having seen any flying buttresses on the house's exterior, but it wouldn't have surprised me if they were there.

Being a bachelor and something of a "neat freak," I always put a lot of effort into keeping my small apartment clean and habitable. Seeing the size of the Dawson mansion, however, made me think of the small army of servants it would require to keep the interior of such a house as immaculate as it appeared. Sure enough, a uniformed servant approached Mr. Dawson and informed him that the planned luncheon was ready to serve. The imperious way Mr. Dawson waved his hand to dismiss the servant really told me something about the kind of person he was: arrogant, demanding, and totally lacking in empathy. At least, that was the impression I had formed of him, and none of his subsequent actions or statements ever convinced me to alter it.

We were quietly ushered into another room that was no less impressive than the one we exited. If I had to choose a one-word, apt description, not only of the room we had just entered but also of any and every other part of the Dawson estate I was allowed to witness, it would be "ornate." I marveled at the attention to detail, from the elegant vases of fresh flowers everywhere down to the hand-carved feet of the cherry-wood display cases. Someone had taken a great deal of time selecting and arranging the decorative objects that adorned the house in various places, as if the tears of a god had fallen to earth and sprouted articles of delicacy and beauty. I was quite sure that the brusque and callous Mr. Dawson had likely played little or no part in this artistry, except, of course, to finance it.

The long, rectangular table in the center, complete with white tablecloth and place settings, announced that we had entered a formal dining room. I wasn't certain if it were "the" dining room; there might have been others scattered elsewhere in the mansion, but I reckoned this enormous one would be more than adequate for our little get-together. The placement of multiple forks, arranged at each setting in a particular order by the size of the utensil, suggested to me, as unsophisticated as I might have been, that I was in a place of exceptional refinement. Here, a wealthy family lived, and they not only knew it, but through their ostentation, they seemed to want everyone else to know it too.

I was not surprised when Mr. Dawson immediately took the chair at one end of the table—what I surmised was its head—and Mrs. Dawson sat to his left. There was an awkward moment when I wasn't sure if Bianca would sit to her father's immediate right or if she would take the chair next to her mother. To my chagrin, and without so much as looking toward me to coordinate, she sat beside her mother, leaving me the only option of the unoccupied side of the table, right next to the glowering patriarch. I wondered if Bianca had simply, out of habit, taken her usual seat at the dinner table, but since she had no siblings, at least any she had told me about, I assumed her facilitating my sitting next to her father for the inevitable paternal grilling was deliberate. *Perhaps she feared his wrath*, I thought, *had she chosen to do otherwise.* Nonetheless, if this were one of the Herculean-type tasks I would have to endure to cement my future with Bianca, I was more than ready to get it started so it could end that much sooner.

As we waited for lunch to be served, I sat uncomfortably in Mr. Dawson's vicinity, his avuncular scowl somehow expanding the sphere of his "personal" space. He turned toward me and said, "Bianca's told me just a few things about you, Mr. Crawford. I'd really like to get to know you better, or perhaps I should say, I want to know more about the most recent fellow my little girl dragged home and happens to be obsessed with this week."

"Daddy!" yelled Bianca, in a tone betraying both hurt and humiliation.

"Please call me 'Trevor,'" I chimed in, so as to ease some of the tension in the air. I looked at the faces around the table; Bianca was still glaring at her father, Mrs. Dawson was demurely looking down, and Mr. Dawson was, as I suspected, transfixed on me. I continued, "Well, I'm sure Bianca's told you that I'm a little younger than her. I just turned twenty-seven a few days ago. And if I had to say one thing about myself, I guess I'd say that I really consider myself to be what some might call a 'people' person."

"By training or by birth?" asked Mr. Dawson.

"Oh, by birth. I've always been that way, as far back as I can remember. And in my job at the bank as a mortgage loan officer I'm constantly meeting new people from all walks of life. In fact, that's how I met your daughter."

"It makes me think," Mr. Dawson said, "I should be more personally involved in handling my affairs."

"Daddy, don't you remember?" Bianca interjected. "I was there to learn more about the business, just like you wanted."

Mr. Dawson turned toward his daughter and said, "Yes, but meeting a clerk at a bank? In person? We have staff for that kind of thing."

Feeling slighted by Mr. Dawson's remarks, I spoke to correct him by saying, "Excuse me, sir, but I'm not a clerk. I handle most of the lending business at the bank, and someday I hope to—"

"Exactly, someday," echoed Mr. Dawson, his voice dripping with contempt as he drawled the word "someday," nearly finding a way to add a syllable. "Have you so little ambition, Mr. Crawford?"

Mrs. Dawson broke her silence and joined the conversation. "Dear, don't you remember, when you were Trevor's age, you were still in school? I recall it well, because I was so thrilled to be dating a college man."

"That's precisely it. Thank you, Elsa, for making my point to Mr. Crawford here. Do you know what I was doing in college? I was working toward my law degree. My goal was to improve my prospects with a real career, not fritter away my time at a bank, shuffling papers."

"Please, Daddy, let's not talk about Trevor's job right now."

"Okay, fair enough. But let me ask you this, Mr. Crawford: In the game of life, are you a buyer or a seller? My experience has shown me that a man cannot be both."

"Well, if I had to pick one," I said, in an effort to buy myself some time to think, "I guess I'm a seller. Since a young age, I've been something of a go-getter. They say that a born salesman—no matter what product he may be peddling—must be able to sell himself to others. So my motto has always been: If you're not selling yourself, then you're selling yourself short."

Mr. Dawson did not visibly react, and if he were planning to reply to me, he was stopped from doing so by the arrival of the luncheon's first course, served by white-gloved attendants who had floated in silence into the dining room through a well-oiled swinging door in the back wall. Because I was unfamiliar with the cuisine being presented, I was too polite to refuse any of the offered courses. Whatever the meal consisted of, it was clear from the sprigs of bright-green parsley, plus the way each entree had been stacked and centered in the plate, that everything had been sumptuously and lovingly prepared. Even to my undiscerning palate, each course was delightfully delicious in its own way.

I had always been aware during our courtship that Bianca ate very little, a practice I had attributed to her generally being finicky about most things. But I noticed that, while her father seemed not to restrict himself, her mother was served remarkably small portions, making me wonder if Bianca had picked up the practice from her. Like any family, the Dawsons had their oddities, in both personalities and behaviors, but seeing each one's idiosyncrasy on open display nonetheless made them all markedly more human in my eyes. But flaws that seem cute initially have a way of becoming grating over time. I wanted Mr. Dawson's blessing, but I wasn't sure I entirely wanted to become part of the Dawson family. Even their wealth felt to me forbiddingly aloof.

Despite being a self-proclaimed "people" person, I tended to take an instant dislike to anyone who refused to open up to me immediately or show some semblance of sociability. Whether due to smugness or shyness—and Mr. Dawson was decidedly the opposite of shy—I always found it difficult to warm up to people who had taken an aloof attitude toward me at the outset, even after I eventually got to know them better. One could call it an uncanny sense, but I seemed invariably to know, within five minutes of meeting someone, if we were destined to end up as friends or as horn-locking enemies. As I sat and listened to Mr. Dawson begin pontificating about the lowly status of the natural salesman that I had just declared myself to be, I didn't have to rely on my intuition to realize that my relationship with my prospective future father-in-law would be, at best, cordial.

Once he figuratively dismounted his high horse, Mr. Dawson changed subjects and asked, "What about your own family? Are they well-established here?"

"Well, I—"

He interrupted me, not so much to ask questions as to make his own commentary. "I'll readily admit that the name 'Crawford' is not altogether uncommon, but I personally haven't encountered it before. Hold on." He turned to his wife and asked, "Elsa, wasn't there something in the newspaper a few weeks ago about a criminal named 'Crawford' or something like that?"

"No, dear," she replied. "I believe that was 'Wilkes.' Not quite the same."

"Yes, quite right," he said, with a tinge of disappointment in his voice.

I decided to chime in with some actual facts. "I was five years old when my Uncle Joe and Aunt Angela became my foster parents. They are my parents, as far as I'm concerned, which is why they asked me from the beginning to call them Mom and Dad. My biological mother, however, is Dad's sister, Alma, or 'Auntie' as I call her."

It was Mrs. Dawson who reacted with astonishment. "You call your own flesh-and-blood mother 'Auntie?'" Her emotional tone and hurt expression made me feel as though I had offended the very concept of motherhood; as a mother herself, she apparently wanted to challenge me over this, more so than her husband, who had remained uncharacteristically quiet during the exchange.

"Well, my parents, that is to say, my foster parents, have two other children, my cousins Matthew and Emily, and since they call Alma by the name of 'Auntie,' that's what we all do. It's actually not as confusing as it sounds and was much less so for a five-year-old."

Mrs. Dawson shook her head and frowned. She might even have clicked her tongue, but with such constraint that it was barely audible. She seemed skeptical, as though unconvinced by the rationale I offered, so I decided to bolster it a bit.

"I've always wanted to come out and say 'mother' to Auntie. I even tried once, but as I recall, she scolded me, and I never tried again." That attempt to clarify only seemed to vex Mrs. Dawson further, as she widened her gaze and looked askance.

At the risk of digging the hole deeper, I continued with my explanation. "Dad's last name—and Auntie's maiden name—is 'Wilkins,' but my biological father's name is 'Crawford,' and that's what I've gone by, even after my foster parents took me in."

The three faces around the table seemed to share a common expression of confusion, as though my statement had equally perplexed them. Mr. Dawson mumbled, nearly under his breath, "Is that another brother of your mother's?" to which Mrs. Dawson admonished him to mind his manners.

Breaking an awkward silence, Mr. Dawson said, "Tell me about your father. I'd like to know, because I happen to believe that it's the best predictor of how a child will grow up." With a grin that seemed eerily maniacal to me, he turned to look across the table at Bianca, who was beaming her lovely smile back at him.

I almost didn't want to disturb the father-daughter connection I was witnessing, but I knew Mr. Dawson wasn't apt to let me off the hook about information he regarded as so important. "Don't know. Never met him. In fact, my birth certificate has Auntie's married name—Alma Crawford—for the mother, but the father's name was just 'Crawford,' so I don't even know his first name. If he's still alive, I kind of hope it's 'Trevor.' I've asked Auntie, my mother, about it, but she won't discuss it with me."

"Then how do you know she was even married?" he asked.

"Well, I guess I don't actually know. She has a career, so I doubt he just knocked her up. I figure she's a widow or a divorcee; all I know is I can't remember ever meeting the guy. The sad fact is that I—and Auntie, for that matter—will both be carrying this man's name with us to the grave."

"I can't imagine marrying a bastard," Bianca said flatly, chuckling to herself. It didn't occur to me at the time how heartless she had been in making such a comment, but even if I had thought about it, I probably would've brushed it off as more a sign of rudeness than contempt. It did not, even for a moment, diminish the love I felt for her. I hoped that, someday when we were married, we'd share a laugh about her insensitive, little snipe about my legitimacy.

I acted as though I hadn't heard Bianca's comment or was choosing to ignore it. "Dad has been a wonderful father, though; he treats me the same as his other kids. I'd be proud to end up like him. If that's my future, then you have nothing to worry about, Mr. Dawson."

"No, I don't agree," Mr. Dawson said. "Elsa's brother happens to be a United States Senator. I'm sure you've heard of Sen. Everett Tillman." I nodded. "How I wish he were my brother. Now, my own brother, on the other hand, is another story altogether. He's what I would call a ne'er-do-well, and that's putting it mildly. If I thought for a minute that my only daughter was going to follow in his footsteps, I'd have smothered her in her crib." He looked up precisely in time to catch Mrs. Dawson's disapproving glare and changed his line of questioning. "Perhaps you met your real father when you were a boy."

"That's the thing. I've heard that most people can remember their childhood back to when they were three or four. For me, my memories begin well past my fifth birthday; anything before that is a blur. And I know I didn't ever meet him as far back as I'm able to remember. Is that a problem for you?"

"What possible problem could I have," Mr. Dawson began, sarcasm dripping from every word, "that my only daughter is seeing a human ATM with no father?"

"Look here, Mr. Dawson: Except for a little musical chairs, I have a great family. If Bianca's as serious about me as I am about her, someday you'll meet my parents and my younger cousins, and you'll see for yourself what wonderful people they are." Mr. Dawson's cowed look demonstrated that he wasn't used to anyone standing up to him, especially those whom he considered inferior, which was pretty much everyone on the planet. Although there would be more grilling to come, I hoped he'd respect me for taking a firm stance in defense of my family and for enduring his overbearing demeanor.

As we continued eating our lunch, I made a special effort to observe each utensil the others were using for each course so I could mimic them and not feel as out-of-place as I truly was. If Bianca and I were fated to be together, this would not be the last time I visited the Dawson estate or ate at one of their immaculate dinner tables or daintily sipped tea, pinkie up, in one of their parlors. I prided myself on having behaved so well and having made it through the worst of the ordeal of confronting, if not yet winning over, Bianca's impossible-to-please father. I was one step closer to making Bianca my wife.

3

Driving away in Matt's car

Matt was only a year younger than me, but he always had a thing for fast cars, and his latest was no exception. Its oversized exhaust pipes, distinctive insignia, and sleek contours were all features which served to announce to any potential passenger that this fine piece of machinery was unmistakably a sports car. It was far from a comfortable ride, but anyone foolish enough to strap into such a "rocket" of a car would know, or should know, that sports cars leave comfort at the curb in a straight trade-off for velocity. Matt had long been fascinated with speed, and he needed a car that would, without falter, supply it. In fact, he had chosen to live in squalor, in a tiny apartment in the crime-ridden side of town, just so he could afford the car payments for his latest speedster. His mom—our mom?—worried that someday his beloved car would end up being his metal coffin. On this evening, however, as we escaped my embarrassing wedding, speed was exactly what we needed.

He shifted the sports car into gear, and we were quickly on the road. To the right, in front of the church,

I saw my own car—the chariot I had planned to ride into happiness—empty tin cans dangling forlornly from its rear.

We drove without saying a word for several miles. The road unfurled in front of us, like a black asphalt carpet, as we hurtled down the highway, not so much toward any particular destination, but away from the site of my monumental mess up. Behind us, the image of the church rapidly shrank, as did my heart, since I had abandoned the love of my life at the proverbial altar.

And in the process, I had wounded not just my bride-to-be but also both our families. My mother, and her brother and sister-in-law who raised me as their foster child, had welcomed Bianca into the family, while Bianca's parents, especially that stone-faced father of hers, had likewise somehow come to accept me, albeit grudgingly at first. Doubtlessly, her parents would be reflexively spitting whenever my name was mentioned, and they would be trying to convince poor Bianca that, based solely on my "performance" at the altar, I was utterly no good for her.

Finally, Matt broke the silence. "What on earth just happened, Trev? Are you freakin' insane?" These were hardly the comforting words I was hoping to hear.

"I dunno, maybe I am," I meekly offered.

"That's the first—no, only—time I've ever seen you lose it like that. Hey, is this your way of dumping her? Because, if it is, then let me tell you, Bro: That's harsh."

The passing scenery had mesmerized me to the point that I nearly fell into a stupor, but Matt's comments struck me like a kick in the head. "No way," I assured him. "First of all, I love Bianca; I'd never do anything to hurt her. And second, if I were going to call it off, do you really think I'd pick the most humiliating way to do it?"

Matt took his eyes off the road momentarily to look me in the face, and the icy logic of my words registered in his expression: His gaze of pained relief, accompanied by a sly smile, warmed me like a hug. It was his way of telling me he would forever be on my side.

As he resumed scanning the dusky road, I sensed he was fumbling in his mind for the right words to say. Finally, he spoke, just above a whisper, "It reminds me of that saying. You know the one: 'No man is an island.'"

I had been waiting to hear words of brotherly compassion. In the absence of those, I would also have welcomed a few words of wisdom, the kind that were forged in the fire of life's experiences; in their own way, such words could provide a form of comfort and bring a sense to one's mind that everything would eventually be all right. Instead, Matt had chosen a seemingly irrelevant truism from another century. I parroted the words, incredulously, "No man is an island?"

Matt smirked as he added, "But some are incontinent."

Because I was so desperate for something—anything—to ground me and make me leave behind the horrors of my aborted wedding, hearing Matt's crude yet affectionate ribbing actually came like a gratifying reprieve. "That's not even a 'wee' bit funny, dude," I replied with a grin.

Matt caught a glimpse of my smile. "I knew we were going to laugh about this someday, but this has got to be some kind of record."

"Poor Bianca," I said, in an effort to remind us both of who the real victim of the day's events had been and who would never share our playful outlook.

"Dude, she's high-maintenance. You knew that going in. Trophies need to be polished; trophy wives are no different."

"Where does that come from? I know you're not speaking from experience. Yet, in a weird way, you do sound pretty wise there, Matt." I paused and then asked, "Do you think she's all right, though? Think she'll get over it?"

"Over it? You mean, over it enough to try to marry your sorry butt again? Hey, I doubt it. I mean, look at her. She could have any man she wanted; why waste her time on Mr. Tinky-Winky here?"

"Can I take back what I said about you being wise? It's not all about appearances. In a lot of ways," I said, almost wistfully, "I pity her."

"Uh, I think you've got that backwards, Bro."

I was aware I was about to launch into lecture mode, so I raised a hand to stop him from trying to teach me something I already knew. I had something to say, and I figured that I needed to hear it—that is, I needed to hear myself speak it aloud—just about as much as Matt needed to hear the life lesson on which it was based. "Coming from a wealthy family, her life has been meticulously ministered, crafted since birth. Her being beautiful merely complicates that, which is why, in an odd way, I really do feel sorry for her."

"Naw, I know that. I mean, that's kinda what I'm saying: She's been rehearsing her wedding day since she was first outta diapers. Don't you get it? You're just a stand-in for the blasted teddy bear she's been marrying the last twenty years. Any guy'll do. It doesn't have to be you."

I couldn't help but wonder how Matt had gotten to be so jaded about life. I tried to recall if I had witnessed anything in his experiences up to that point to account for it. *Had I somehow missed an event,* I thought, *like a bad prom date or an unfaithful ex-girlfriend*? This wasn't the time to straighten him out, but I promised myself that, once my own wedding fiasco was resolved, I would help mend Matt's heart so he would again be open to the idea of love.

I reaffirmed my own short-term goal: resolving the wedding fiasco I had created. Unfortunately, I had no idea how to even begin doing that. Not only did I not have a plan for getting everyone together so I could talk to them, but even if I got them in the same room at the same time, I had no way to explain my bizarre behavior. I felt that I just needed time to think. I went back to my usual mantra, that I considered myself a man of reason. Surely, the answers would come to me, even if I were drawing a blank at that moment.

The sun had disappeared below the horizon, and I couldn't help but think that, but for my un-explained blunder at the altar, I would already be married, enjoying the fruits of wedded bliss. Speeding down the dark highway as a passenger in Matt's car was not helping me come up with a plan, but I nonetheless took solace in it. Hurtling into the unknown felt like a metaphor and it proved to be just the beginning of an ordeal that, like the asphalt, lay menacingly before me.

4

Calling the preacher

After the fiasco at the church, I knew I would eventually have to make contact with the Dawsons, but I dreaded even the thought of it. Mrs. Dawson, as usual, would say nothing, but Mr. Dawson would be screaming for my head on a platter. If someday everything calmed down and we actually tried to stage another wedding, whom could he invite? The same crowd of 500 well-heeled acquaintances he encountered—and would continue to encounter—in his elite, upper-crust circles? The same ones who had brought their pretentious wedding gifts to the church and who were right then probably tsk-tsking poor Bianca's impulsive choice for a fiancé, a man who would never fit into their world.

What about poor Bianca? How could she try to marry me again, or any one, in that church or any other within a thousand miles? More importantly, why would she? I had ruined beyond all repair, not merely her special day, but in many ways, her whole, perfectly planned and orchestrated life. I pondered the ramifications: *Had I actually abandoned her at the altar?* If it weren't abandonment, what else could one call it?

I felt helpless. This had not been an error in judgment or a failure in execution. If the task had been a physical one, say, to jump ten feet in the air from a running start, and if I had only jumped nine feet, at least the effort would have been there, and in such a case, I would have fallen short due to my own limitations. But what had this been, this soiling myself for no apparent reason in front of a crowd of well-wishers? Would everyone assume I had done it on purpose? As in, *"Here's what I think of your elitism, you snobs."* But it wasn't deliberate. Surely, upon reflection, they would all realize that.

So, Bianca's fiancé got a little nervous. He had a little accident. Was that enough to put an end to what might have grown into a lifetime of happiness? *Blast it all, why did I have to pick the white tuxedo?*

Okay, if I were going to make an attempt at recovery, of redeeming myself and begging forgiveness from every person in that cathedral-sized church, I had to make a list. And who would be at the top of that list? My instinct told me it should be Bianca. Yet, I had little doubt she was being alternately berated and consoled by her adoring albeit menacing father. "There, there, little girl," he would be saying, as he patronizingly patted her shoulder. "But how could you embarrass us by wanting to marry that leaky bank teller? If I ever get a hold of his spigot—"

No, as much as I wanted to call Bianca and remind her that the only thing that mattered was our love for each other, I could not stomach the thought of Mr. Dawson screaming in the background, yelling for my head. I'd have to let Bianca's emotions settle down, and then I would call her.

I tried to think of someone who was a neutral party in all this and who might even serve as a liaison to the Dawsons, someone who could soften them up for me until I had the nerve to approach them again. It was the pastor, Rev. Harrington. Moreover, as a man of God, he would have to have pity on me. The Dawsons were the ones who were Presbyterian, but I was sure their priest understood the frailties of mankind: *The flesh is weak,* and all that. Wasn't the bladder made of flesh? For my sake, I hoped so.

From the wedding planner's list of contacts, I had Rev. Harrington's telephone number handy and decided to call him immediately. He would be able to tell me how people had initially reacted to my little incident and whether any of the resulting tumult had died down. He answered the phone on the first ring. I found his greeting, "Rev. Harrington at your service," in his booming stentorian baritone, to be quite comforting.

"Reverend, this is Trevor Crawford," I said. Given that it had only been a matter of hours since the episode, it felt a little odd making such a formal introduction. *What else was I going to say? "Forgive me, Father, for I have peed," perhaps? Best to keep this professional.*

A tense silence on the other end ensued. "My dear Mr. Crawford, I was hoping to hear from you. The guests were quite worried about you. I always tell my parishioners that there's never a need to run away. Our Lord is beside us and will comfort us in our times of need."

"I really have no explanation for what happened. What I needed was some time to figure out what I've done. But I thought it was important to call you—"

"You did the right thing, my son. I am sure you want to know how things stand. The Dawsons were very gracious and put everyone at ease. When the church was clearing out, there was more concern for you than any bitterness."

"But they did realize it was an accident, didn't they? I hope they didn't think—"

"No, the general consensus, as I read it, was an unfortunate case of nerves. I often see cold feet, especially among the grooms, although I must say, in my twenty-five years in the ministry, this was truly a first."

"What now?" I asked. "If Bianca and I decide to try this again, will we have your support, as well as the support of the church?"

"I think you will find us church folk to be a forgiving bunch. That was a little church humor, by the way. You need to remember that it is not just a decision for you and the bride. Marriage is a covenant with God." Rev. Harrington paused before interjecting, "Are you still there?"

"Yes, Reverend, a covenant with God." The thought briefly entered my mind that, if bringing about this marriage from the outset were somehow God's doing, why would He have chosen that moment in time to humiliate me? Maybe I needed some humility. If so, He should have just punished me, rather than embarrass my beloved, her family, and everyone at that church. But I had to expect that this priest was going to bring God into all of this, since that was his business. "Go on," I urged him.

"The esteemed state of Holy Matrimony—" he began to say. As soon as the words reached my ear, pressed against the telephone receiver, that same sense of dread that had overcome me at the church swept over me again. My body stiffened, and I was seized with an utterly uncontrollable urge, like a reflex, to urinate. I looked downward at my lap, and, even through the rough denim of my jeans, I saw a tiny darkened circle swell into a giant wet spot. To my own amazement, I had soiled myself again.

The nauseating dizziness and overall numbness had become somewhat familiar sensations. If only I could understand why this was happening, then I would have had a chance to fight against it. Instead, I sat in humiliating indignity for the second time in the same day. At least this time, there were no witnesses to see it.

Could I have been drugged? I wondered. If that were the case, my suspicions would fall immediately on Mr. Dawson. Not only had he made it clear that he never liked me, but a man of his wealth would have the means to carry out such a diabolical plot to humiliate me and ensure I'd never be part of his family. *But then again, no*, I concluded: Mr. Dawson loved his daughter more than he hated me, and he would never do anything to embarrass or hurt her feelings. It had been an interesting notion, but the riddle of my uncontrollable behavior remained a mystery.

"Reverend, I'm getting another call," I lied, "and I think it's Bianca. I'm going to have to call you back. Thank you for your counsel and understanding."

"All right, but—"

I didn't let him finish before disconnecting. I called out to Matt, who was in the next room. When he came in, I was surprised how quickly he assessed the situation and left the room immediately without saying a word; I didn't know if he had run off in disgust or had gone to retrieve another set of clothes for me.

Sitting alone in silence, I wasn't sure which made me more uncomfortable: the sinking sense of degradation I felt or the unwelcome sensation of untimely moisture. I allowed my thoughts to wander and to transport me away from the situation in which I found myself. I recalled the fib I had just told to end my conversation with Rev. Harrington, namely, that Bianca was calling me. *Why hadn't she called me yet?* I wondered. I desperately wanted to talk to her, to tell her that my feelings for her hadn't changed and that we still had a bright future together. My thoughts inevitably returned to the present circumstances, and it became clear that I could not—no, I would not—bring myself to call Bianca until I had gotten control of my problem, or at least understood it. I had to be able to look her in the eye with confidence and without worrying that I might spontaneously debase myself. Until that day, however, I would have to endure her absence and patiently wait for her to make the decision to contact me.

Matt returned, and as he handed me the fresh pair of trousers, I wanted to cry. Instead, I asked wearily and almost rhetorically, "Why is this happening to me?"

"Dude, you may not want to hear it, but it's time for you to see a doctor. You said you felt fine physically, so if that's the case, I'm thinking we'd best find you a head-shrinker. Pronto!"

5

Seeking a psychologist

Matt was right about my needing help, and if the help I needed had to come from a psychiatrist, then I was prepared to seek one out, no matter the cost to purse or pride. Bizarre behavior could be terribly unsettling, not simply because one tended to act completely out-of-character, but because there was no telling what one might do at the next unguarded moment. *What if, instead of a bladder issue, I suddenly became homicidal?* The loss of even a little control could be maddening, since it might portend the loss of complete control. I wasn't so concerned about the urination response itself—that was what adult diapers were for—but as soon as I managed to patch that problem, I wondered what would be next. I knew there was little point in medicating a symptom while allowing its cause to go untreated.

I pondered the feeling of dread that seemed to precipitate the symptom, and then it occurred to me that both these two incidents in the same day did seem to be some kind of reaction to something. One involved a crowd and the other a private telephone call. In that way, they were totally different. On the other hand and no less mysteriously, both involved Rev. Harrington in various capacities. Even though he was the priest in Bianca's church, and I had only known him during our time planning the wedding arrangements, he seemed a nice enough man. He was firm, yet gentle. In fact, I had grown to like him on a personal level. *How could my behavior be triggered by, or in any way involve, a man I so liked and admired?* At least on first inspection, it didn't make any sense.

I did feel fine physically. I frequented the neighborhood gym on a regular basis and had felt no ill effects of even strenuous workouts. Nonetheless, the human body—and the human mind, for that matter—has long been considered a complex system, which means that the breakdown of any one of its components might lead to a complete systemic failure. I could have speculated all sorts of explanations for my periodic incontinence, but I instead decided to see my family doctor at the first opportunity. I had to lie to the receptionist over the phone that it was an emergency; that was the only way his office would squeeze me into his tight schedule. *Didn't botching your own wedding and potentially losing your fiancée qualify as an emergency, if not medically, then at least psychologically?* That was how I justified my little fib, and it worked. I saw my physician later that same afternoon.

A cursory yet probing examination failed to reveal any physical cause for my humiliating behavior. In fact, my doctor was very clear that, for a man a week away from his twenty-ninth birthday, I was the picture of health. If I had a problem, it was decidedly located just north of the neckline. The good doctor wrote a referral for me to see a specialist. It was not, however, to a urologist; no, it was indeed for what Matt insensitively called a "head shrinker." If I felt any initial embarrassment, it vanished as soon as it became clear that I was beset with a problem worth looking into and had chosen to do something about it.

The written referral included a telephone number for the National Psychological Organization, or NPO. I couldn't help but wonder if this was the type of referral my doctor often found himself making for his patients. I was aware that society tends to view those with mental issues as anomalies, but maybe being sane in a world as crazy as this one could be itself a form of insanity. Here I was, a few days removed from when I was to have been married and starting on a new, exciting life with a beautiful wife, and instead, I was cold calling to make an appointment with a psychoanalyst. Considering what I had just given up, it didn't seem all that inappropriate after all.

It started to dawn on me, though, that none of the Dawson family had even attempted to contact me. My heart sank as I thought of Bianca. The last time I had seen her, she was crying, sobbing actually, in that crowded church. Why hadn't she called or texted me? Was what I had done so unforgivable? She lacked for nothing except some space, and while I was busy preparing to delve into my psyche, I was more than willing to afford her that time away from me. Still, why hadn't her father at least left me a voicemail message, or, as was more his style, written me a stern letter, excoriating me for having humiliated him, his daughter, his whole family, not to mention myself and the entire county where the church was situated? Sometimes the deliberate withholding of punishment can feel like the severest blow of all. I began to wonder if I would ever hear from a Dawson or hear their names spoken in my presence ever again.

I decided my first family contact, aside from Matt, would be my mother, Aunt Alma, or "Auntie," as we all called her. Since Matt was sitting next to me, I used the telephone's speaker, which was not what I normally would do, considering how I had planned to talk about some embarrassing stuff. But Matt was like a brother to me, and I thought he'd agree that my problems were his problems, and vice versa. As I dialed the number of her cell phone, I had the strangest feeling that she was somehow expecting my call at that precise moment. She answered on the first ring. "Auntie," I said immediately upon connecting and without waiting for the customary hello, "it's Trevor."

"Sweet boy, why did it take so long for you to call me? I wanted to give you some space, so of course I held off calling you, but I am your mother, after all. You can tell me anything. What's going on, dear one?"

"I'm here with Matt, and I'm having a problem. Well, duh. I'm not only embarrassed; frankly, I'm getting kind of scared. Something is happening to me. I don't know why I do the things I do."

"Oh, Trevor, I'm sure everything is fine. I believe you didn't want to go through with the wedding, and you just had an interesting way of postponing it, that's all."

"Auntie, it's Matt here—I know you love Trevor—"

"Matt, I love you, too. Don't forget that. Right now, Trevor has our attention, but you and Emily are as close to my heart as any niece and nephew could be."

"Love you, too, Auntie," Matt said. "I'm not trying to be your favorite nephew here, but we've got to work together and get Trevor some help."

"It's true, Auntie," I interjected. "I got a referral to see a psychologist or psychiatrist or whatever, and well, I think I'm going to go ahead and pursue that. If I can get my head on straight, maybe, I hope, Bianca will take me back."

"Have you called Bianca yet?"

I remembered the pledge I had made to myself after the second incident to not even attempt to call Bianca until I had a handle on things. I didn't share the details of my pledge but replied, "No. I was hoping you or someone in the family had spoken with her or her parents. Have you?"

"What's important is that you get the help you need."

"That's what I've been telling him," Matt asserted.

"Do you recall when you were a boy, Trevor, you sought my help after you had seen eight cartoons straight of Bugs Bunny, and you were so disoriented?"

"No, I can't say I remember that happening, but in a weird way, it does kind of ring a bell. Did you help me?"

"Of course. Back then, I was still a full-time, practicing psychologist, the only woman at the time working at the old clinic who had earned a professional degree. Wow, that must be, what, over twenty years ago?"

"So, can you help me now?"

"I hung up my lab coat a long time ago," she said. "I do occasionally consult, but I wouldn't dream of treating anyone from start to finish anymore, least of all my own flesh-and-blood."

"Okay, but do you still happen to know any of the psychologists you used to work with who might be able to help me?"

"The old clinic was shuttered, but there's the new one they opened down on Fourth Street off Main. I don't know anyone there, but this is your decision anyway: You need to see a therapist who understands you and makes you comfortable. Do not just go with the first one you happen to find."

"I won't, Auntie. Thanks for the support. I'm not sure I could make it through this ordeal without you and Matt. I'll call you when I've found a therapist. But in the meantime, promise me something."

She asked, "What's that?"

"Don't worry about me."

"I most certainly will not promise you that. A mother always worries about her children. But do keep me posted. And let me know if there's anything I can do for you, son."

"I will. Bye."

"Bye, Auntie," Matt chimed in, before I disconnected.

I briefly thought about going to the new clinic in person and seeing who there could take me as a new patient. But I decided instead to call the NPO referral number my medical doctor had given me. I expected the National Psychological Organization to be as professional as their name suggested and that they would hook me up with a suitable therapist. I was hoping it just might be with someone at the clinic after all. *How many therapists could there be in town anyway?* I thought. Going through official channels, as recommended by my doctor, seemed a better approach than simply showing up off the street at the clinic.

I was somewhat disappointed, however, when the NPO sent me first to a hospital doctor's office. When that didn't work out, I was forced to wait for them again on account of the holiday. In the interim, I "celebrated" the last birthday of my twenties and put on a brave face so as not to concern anyone. Auntie and Matt knew I was actively seeking help, but they were the only ones and I trusted them to keep it confidential. I stayed up past midnight on my birthday, hoping Bianca would call, but she never did. When I finally went to bed, my eyes ached from holding back the tears. I had to figure that when a man's fiancée forgets his birthday—whether intentionally or not—it can't be a good sign for the health of their relationship. *Maybe if she had known*, I rationalized to myself, *that I was trying to get some help, she would have reached out to me, especially on my birthday.* Instead, I continued my waiting game with the NPO folks.

After more than a week, they finally arranged for me to visit another outpatient clinic across town, with more potential psychologists assigned there. All of them were of different backgrounds, demeanors, methods, and walks of life. Who knew the town I called home was such a throbbing mass of hurt that it would require the services of such an army of Freudians? Life could be a painful series of events, more for some than for others, but I had always been confident I could soldier on through it with nothing more than my wits and cynical sense of humor. How had a lucrative industry emerged whose essence was a consoling pat on the back for folks overwhelmed by life's ceaseless setbacks? And yet, there I was, in a quest for help from just such a back-patter. *Was that something I really needed?* If I imagined scores of people peeing their pants across town, then I could better make sense of the dozens of psychologist offering to help them. Surely, no one had a worse problem than that.

None of the handful of psychologists to whom I had been referred up to that point personally appealed to me, and none gave me any prospect of being able genuinely to help me. The one at the hospital looked haggard, both of his eyelids drooping, as if he were in a constant struggle to stay awake, and his face was frozen in a perpetual expression of surly indifference; whether his exhaustion was due to being overworked, I couldn't say, but he gave me the sense that he was doing me a huge favor by taking time out of his busy schedule to listen to me and my problems. Another one, the first at the uptown clinic, was a bespectacled, aging gentleman with a beard and thin, ominously long fingers; he suggested a prolonged and expensive treatment focused on problems rooted in early childhood. The second at the same clinic was a woman who betrayed her professionalism—yet revealed her humanity—by visibly trying to suppress a chortle every time I mentioned my embarrassing bladder incidents. A third, whom I never actually saw, kept postponing my appointment; in disappointment, I canceled seeing him after the third postponement in as many weeks. It became clear to me that none of these therapists were equipped on any level to solve my problem.

When I called the NPO for a fifth time, I made it clear that I didn't want to waste any more time and asked specifically if they could refer me to the downtown clinic with which Auntie had been loosely associated. The NPO referral service operator explained that this was not how it worked. She said she understood my frustration, and she was prepared to give me the next name on the list, but I could not make a request by location. Otherwise, she explained, the folks in the other locations might never get a referral. I wondered to myself, *"Is that my problem?"* But with their take-it-or-leave-it attitude, I decided to just go to the new clinic myself and ask around.

Matt accompanied me to the new clinic, and when we arrived, we immediately went to the large directory just inside the foyer. The white-lettered names and room numbers were aligned with precision on the black, velvety background. I scanned the dozen or so names but then went back to one that had instantly caught my eye: Dr. Nathan Carr. I seemed to want to pronounce it as "Nate Carr" but was sure it would be "Dr. Carr" if I were ever to establish a relationship with him.

For Matt's benefit, I put my finger next to the name and started walking toward the indicated office. When we entered the waiting room, it was well-lit but smelled oddly musty. Matt staked out a seat in a chair in the far corner and began to leaf through some old magazines. I felt a bit abandoned, but I figured he was only along with me to provide a little moral support.

The receptionist's counter had a small ledge, above which was a frosted-glass sliding window that happened to be closed shut as I approached it. I saw behind the window the silhouette of a woman, apparently primping her hair, standing at a distance of what must have been a few feet on her side of the counter. The silhouette descended, as if sitting at a chair just behind the window, which slid abruptly open to reveal the face of a woman—frowning, but otherwise bereft of emotion—who stared at me without flinching. I spoke to her through the opening.

"I'd like to make an appointment with Dr. Carr, please," I announced. The waiting room was empty, except for Matt, sitting in the corner, absorbed with looking through the magazines.

"Sir, not so loud," the receptionist said. I'm not sure if she thought Matt was another potential patient, but I nodded to signal that I agreed to speak in hushed tones from then on.

"In any case," she continued, "Dr. Carr is on a sabbatical this month."

"Oh," I said; if words could form a frown, my words dripped with disappointment. "Is he referring any of his patients to someone else?"

"We have a replacement psychiatrist working in the office here, Dr. Gustav Romero. Do you still want to make an appointment to see him?"

"Yes, please."

She averted her gaze to look at a desktop calendar that I squinted to see over the rim of the counter. From my obstructed vantage, it looked bereft of any writing whatsoever, as if no appointments had been recorded. "The doctor is available now, if you'd like to start immediately."

"I have someone with me," I said, as I gestured toward Matt, still absorbed in scanning the magazines. "Could it be another day?"

"Would ten o'clock tomorrow morning work for you?"

"Yes, it would, indeed."

"Please fill out this paperwork and insurance forms," she said, with a matter-of-fact air of efficiency, as she handed me a clipboard with a dauntingly thick sheaf of papers attached. She then whisked the window shut again. I sat next to Matt and began filling out the forms.

Okay, Gustav Romero—not the one I wanted to see, but I could deal with that. The name sounded vaguely European; Vienna, after all, was the birthplace of psychoanalysis. Maybe he could do all the ground-work to hand over to Dr. Carr upon his return.

I filled out the forms, which were pretty much the standard boilerplate stuff: contact information, allergies, medications, legal disclosures, etc. I turned to ask, "Hey, Matt, are you okay if I list you as my contact?"

"Sure, but why aren't you using Bianca's… Oh, right. Sorry. Go ahead."

I couldn't tell if Matt was being sarcastic or had genuinely forgotten that I hadn't seen my fiancée in weeks—*had it slipped his mind why I was even seeing a head-shrinker?*—so I chose to ignore his remark. As a mortgage loan officer, I was used to rapidly filling out forms, so I hastily finished the paperwork and walked back to the reception window. Almost as if on cue, the receptionist re-opened the counter window and accepted the clipboard from me with the completed forms. I noticed a cradle of business cards on the counter.

As I readied to pick one of the cards, I noticed it was for Dr. Carr. I asked the receptionist if Dr. Romero had a business card I could take with me. She acted annoyed at my request, reached around with her left hand from behind the counter to retrieve a business card from the cradle, and wrote in broad strokes a phone number on the back of the card before handing it to me. "That's Dr. Romero's cell phone number," she said.

I took the card, and as I was thanking her, she curtly snapped, "See you tomorrow, Mr. Crawford," before once more sliding the fogged divider shut. I hoped Dr. Romero had a better bedside manner than what I had seen so far. I was desperate and was sure he would be able to help me. After all, I would be entrusting him not only with my confidential matters but also, in a sense, with my very sanity.

6

Visiting Dr. Romero

The next morning came, and promptly at ten o'clock, I found myself at the clinic, in the hallway, staring at Dr. Romero's office door. There was something sterile and uninviting about the door: Through it, I hoped to solve the mystery concerning my recent behavior, but I also harbored reservations, with the thought that perhaps I would be better off not knowing the answer. *If a sign appeared that read "This way happiness" and another, pointing the other direction, that read "This way despair," what sane person, without hesitation, would so much as consider following the latter, even if it offered a comforting sense of closure? Yet, didn't there dwell within every human being a deep desire—a child-like, insatiable curiosity—that demanded answers to every question posed by life, especially the ones concerning the important matters that affect our happiness?* Once I determined, for the sake of my future with Bianca, that I needed to know the answer to the particular question concerning my psychological well-being, I gripped the doorknob, turned it with a fierce determination, and strode confidently through what, at that moment, seemed to represent the very portal of my own sanity.

The receptionist must have heard me open the door, because she shoved the frosted window above her counter to one side and peered out into the empty waiting room. I informed her that I was there for my appointment to see Dr. Romero. A night's sleep hadn't softened her demeanor. She was all business. Some might call this simply being professional, but in my time working at the bank, I had come to realize that less-than-friendly people were usually hiding something. She pressed the buzzer to unlock the inner door and gestured for me to enter. In my imagination, I had expected her to come around, take me by the hand, and usher me into the therapy room. Instead, I put one foot in front of the other and marched into the room unassisted, not knowing what to expect.

What I noticed first was an older man seated behind a desk, and he indicated to me with a hand gesture that I could sit in either of two empty chairs, one in front of the desk or the other on the side. The door had quietly shut itself behind me.

"I'm Dr. Romero," he intoned formally, offering to shake my hand. We shook, and he asked, "How may I help you?"

"I think I need some psychological help here, Doc," I said.

"It is a well-established fact in my profession, Mr. Crawford, that everyone can benefit from an examination of one's psyche. Why is it that we take for granted that our bodies need attendance in the form of annual physicals, but our minds are supposed to hum along unexamined for decades?"

"Sorry, Doc, but I'm not here to examine my mind."

"Why do you think you're here then? Or perhaps more properly, let me ask, what brings you here to my office?"

"There's been some strange behavior lately. I want it to stop. I don't really care why it's happening, so long as I can control it. It's been a source of extreme embarrassment for me."

"Well, my expertise is founded on the insight that human beings do not behave strangely without having some psychological reason, so stopping it, as you say, very much involves first understanding the cause and then secondly, either removing the cause or adapting a different response to it. Are you prepared, Mr. Crawford, to delve deeply into your own psyche so we can identify the cause or causes of your behavior?"

"If that's what you think needs to happen, I'm prepared for that. I'll do whatever it takes. But, say... Don't you need to know what the behavior is that I'm talking about?"

"I am not enforcing social norms here, Mr. Crawford. If you believe it is strange and it is causing you discomfort, then my role is to help you come to terms with it. If, say, buttoning your shirt every morning—a seemingly routine and mundane task—were inducing anxiety, it doesn't matter that the act itself is quite normal; my duty is to put your mind at ease so you can go about doing the tasks you have to do and withstand the vagaries of a modern-day, stressful life."

"Nothing is exactly stressing me out. I've done something that may have cost me my fiancée and my future happiness. Is that the kind of thing you can fix?"

"You haven't given any clue as to what it is that you've done, but I can assure you, while I cannot guarantee happiness—such a warranty would be professionally unethical—I can promise that with the therapy I perform, you will be a much better-adjusted person who is thereby more able to be happy under any circumstance. But before I take you on as a patient, I must make you aware of my rather unorthodox methods. I rely almost exclusively on hypno-therapy. Are you familiar with that technique?"

"No, Doc. I vaguely recall having heard of it, probably on TV or in the movies, but I can't say I know anything about it. Is it dangerous?"

"Not unless you're afraid of curing your condition. In that sense, it would be dangerous." He smiled, seemingly to himself. "So, I take it you have not undergone this type of treatment before."

"Can't say that I have. Actually, what am I saying? Let me answer your question frankly: No, I haven't been hypnotized before. In fact, this is the first time I've ever been to a psychologist. If this is a quick cure, though, it may well be my last time."

"I am afraid, Mr. Crawford, I must disabuse you of that notion. There is no 'quick cure' when it comes to healing a diseased mind. The process could take weeks, months, or even years. If you cannot commit to participating fully in your own recovery, then I have no choice but to bid you good day."

"That's harsh, Dr. Romero. I thought therapists were more comforting than that. But I do understand the concern: If a patient doesn't want to be cured, why even begin the process? Okay, Doc. You got me. What do we do next?"

"I could begin by asking you to tell me more about the situation, but in my experience, it is far more efficient to communicate directly with the subconscious mind, since it is the area of your mind likely hosting the troubling thoughts that are generating the behavior you find so problematic. Let's get you under immediately."

Dr. Romero reached into his desk and pulled out a small object. In the strangest way, even though I was directly looking at—or rather, into—the object, I was somehow not actually seeing it. It was like looking down a darkened well. The sensation it produced was akin to the vertigo one might experience while perched on a platform at a very high altitude. Dr. Romero's soothing voice lulled me into embracing the sleepiness he was suggesting, and despite my genuine effort to remain awake, I fell into the blissful slumber that I sensed was the mental state for which he was striving.

Whether or not there was a clock in the therapy room, I could not say, but even if there were, I was utterly unaware of it or any sense of time passing. I would not hazard a guess as to how long I was in my induced hypnotic state, because when I awakened and gathered my wits, it seemed as though mere seconds—at most, a minute or two—had elapsed from when I lost consciousness. As I doubt my dormancy could have actually been so brief, it might well have been hours. My head felt like it weighed a hundred pounds, and, in a dream-like stupor, I slid the left cuff of my shirt aside to read my wristwatch. The LED colon pounded like a hammer the current time: ten forty-five. This confirmed that I had been "under" for about half-an-hour. *Could it have been twenty-four and a half hours?* No, the day of the month dial on my watch showed it was still the same day. And it was past the month I was to have married Bianca, but instead of bathing in wedded bliss, I was sitting in a cold office having my head examined. *What had I revealed to Dr. Romero and what were the results of any analysis he might have made?* I wondered. I spoke and couldn't resist the opportunity, given that I had grown up watching all those Bugs Bunny cartoons.

"What's up, Doc?"

"For your own safety, Mr. Crawford, I have made a post-hypnotic suggestion that you not consciously recall the session we've just had. In my experience, the conscious mind often sabotages the progress I can make dealing directly with the subconscious. When the time comes, and a full recovery of your condition has been initiated, I will then permit retrieval of the memory. Until then, I ask that you try not to interfere with the treatment and keep our sessions confidential."

"Uh, I'm really having a problem with that, Doc. I didn't come here for some paternalistic, father-knows-best nonsense. I need help, and either I'm involved in my own healing, or I may have to find another therapist."

"I wouldn't normally reveal this to a patient, but in my diagnosis, I've concluded that you're not altogether mentally stable, Mr. Crawford. Do not do anything rash. I completely understand your concerns. Do you know anything about a psychological concept called 'classic behavioral conditioning'?"

Hearing the phrase evoked memories of my college days, sitting in some vast lecture hall for the required "Introduction to Psychology" course. I knew what conditioning was, and the distinction between the classical and the operant kinds—one involved a neutral signal that occurred before a reflex, while the other afterward reinforced or punished a particular behavior. I couldn't quite recall which was which, but I decided to encourage Dr. Romero to explain it to me by playing a little dumb about the subject. "Heard of it but don't know much about it."

"I have already set up a demonstration for you. If you can find someone other than me to say the word 'taco' to you directly, be sure to take a seat within the following five minutes, because it will knock you off your feet. Hearing that word will trigger a one-time recollection of a vivid memory from your childhood that was brought out in our session. After that experience, in which you will discover that we have indeed met before, Mr. Crawford, you can decide at that time whether we should continue together exploring your damaged psyche. I want to help you, I really do, but you need to trust me first. I hope this is the foundation on which such a trust can be built."

"I dunno, Doc. This whole arrangement makes me feel kinda agitated."

Dr. Romero reached for a prescription pad on his desk, and as he began writing, he said, "I will prescribe this anti-anxiety medication for you. Only take it if you need to, though." He tore off the top sheet and handed it to me, saying "Have this filled at your local pharmacy. Let me know how things are going. We're going to cure you, Mr. Crawford. I can promise you that."

I took the original prescription, nodded without saying a word, and wandered out of the room. I passed by the reception area. The movement of her silhouette showed the receptionist was just taking her seat, but when the frosted window slid open, she was apparently on the telephone. I didn't know if she might already be phoning in my prescription or was somehow on another call. I chose not to speak with her but walked right on by. I wasn't sure if I even wanted to make another appointment because I really didn't know if I would be back to see Dr. Romero ever again. He seemed nice: He had a comforting if strangely familiar voice, and it appeared from what I had seen that he genuinely wanted to help me. But he was so right, that if we were going to continue together, I would have to learn to trust him. I decided, as a first step, to pursue his little "taco" test before making a final decision.

7

Having lunch at the taco joint

Lunchtime had rolled around, and I was eager to fulfill Dr. Romero's conditioning test as soon as possible. What better way, I reckoned, than to have a meal at one of my favorite restaurants, a little, dimly lit dive by the name of "Tacos Ahora" in the industrial part of town?

I was lucky to find a parking space so near the restaurant during the noon hour. I knew the location, having eaten there many times before, but bizarrely, the sign above the joint read simply "Ahora," with a blank space where the word "Tacos" had been. I wondered if they had changed the name to appeal to a wider clientele. I entered, and the atmosphere was reminiscent of a pool hall: dank, and more than a little bit cold, but strangely inviting and comfortable.

The apron-clad man behind the counter was smiling, and as he looked directly at me while I walked up to place an order, he asked, "What'll you have, sir?"

The mental image of a taco was firmly in my mental grasp, but for some reason, I found myself unable to verbalize it. I figured Dr. Romero had placed a mental block to make it less likely I could get someone to say the word "taco" to me, which was, as he had explained, the sole trigger for me to relive some repressed memory. I thought how ridiculous this exercise was. *In fact, how did I know it wasn't Romero himself in the first place who had suppressed the memory I was now trying to evoke?* No matter what I thought or tried to think, the word simply would not bubble up to my lips.

The man behind the counter continued to smile, although it had become more of a nervous expression than a friendly one. "We have many items to choose from," he offered, possibly in an effort to help me. I looked up at the menu on the wall, and there were huge square areas of blank space; it occurred to me that my mental block somehow encompassed my vision as well. If so, that would also explain the apparently blank space on the sign out front.

I became frightened. I began to sense that all my experiences of the world were merely perceptions. If a simple, post-hypnotic suggestion like the one Dr. Romero had used could alter in every detail how I interpreted those perceptions, even the objective ones, then I could no longer claim to be my own person. Maybe all I needed was to refocus. Surely, over time, I would—as much as this sounded like a pun—come to my senses.

"Yeah, I'll have a double-item combination meal with a soda," I told the man behind the counter, who seemed noticeably relieved that I was finally placing an order after such an awkward delay.

"Okay, sir. What entree would you like?"

"Um, a tortilla thing."

"Do you mean a burrito?"

"No, with the hard shell."

"Okay, one meal-combo tostada. Will that be all, sir?"

"No, no," I said, repeating the negative for emphasis, while noticing that the volume of my voice had risen in frustration. After a brief pause, I resumed in a more muted tone, "It's like that, like a tostada, but I mean with the stuff inside; you know, inside of it."

"Oh, you mean a tacquito." He began to push buttons on the cash register.

"For the love of—" I bit my lip. "Open-faced, like a sandwich."

The man wiped his hands nervously on his apron. "Do you mean our signature dish?" he asked.

"Yes?" I said, as I eagerly anticipated hearing the sought-after word actually spoken out loud.

"A—"

"Yes?"

"Taco?"

"Yes, yes, oh, yes. That is so what I want. I can't tell you how much I want a blessed taco." He looked quizzically at me and eyed the two or three customers who were waiting impatiently behind me. He handed me the receipt with the order number in large lettering at the center; I threw some cash and coins down on the counter, took the empty soda cup he offered me, and walked to an empty table.

I sat and nervously checked my watch, noting what time it would be when, according to Dr. Romero, the anticipated five minutes should have elapsed. Like watching a pot of water come to a boil, the five-minute wait seemed inhumanly interminable. During one of the moments when I was looking out into the room and not at my watch, it came to me. I had a vision, where the place I was physically sitting appeared to melt away. The sounds in the room—the clattering of dishes and the indistinct voices of people conversing at lunch— also turned into an absolute and eerie silence. It was a memory, to be sure, but its vivid recall was more like an hallucinogenic episode than a calm recollection. From what I understood, a mind cannot easily withstand the flood of sensations associated with a repressed memory coming to the fore because it appears like an entirely new event, outside the realm of experience, as if the mind were peering into an undiscovered world. That was how my memory overwhelmed me at that moment.

I had heard that most people could remember their childhood back to when they were four, or three, or even earlier. I had no memories before I was about five-and-a-half years of age. The episode I was reliving counted as among my earliest, from about just around age five or so. It was a few months after my Uncle Joe and Aunt Angela had agreed to foster me. I'd always considered them my parents, which was why it was easy to form the habit, as they insisted, of calling them Mom and Dad, exactly as their own children did.

I was told early on that Dad's sister, Alma, had actually given birth to me. Since as far back as I could remember, my cousins Matt and Emily have called Alma by the name "Auntie," and to avoid confusing the whole family, she asked me to do the same. The one time I called her by the name "mother," Auntie reprimanded me without mercy about it, so I never did try that again. The whole "Auntie" thing used to bother me, but only when I thought about it. Dad was always such a wonderful father, treating me exactly the same as his other kids—Matt, a year younger than me, and Emily, a year younger than Matt—that it never really mattered to me from whose loins I sprang.

Of course, I developed a very special relationship with my cousins: Matt has always been—and I'd venture to guess, always will be—my best friend in the world. And as for Emily, well, she'll forever more be my first romantic interest, even if that didn't turn out quite so well; without her brazen independence and feisty spirit, I doubt I'd have been attracted to my eventual fiancée, Bianca.

Despite our flaws, my family was great, and it would never occur to me to stop defending them because, above all, they made me feel loved, mostly. That was why the memory I was experiencing, while sitting in that dark, little taco joint, stood in stark contrast as an embarrassing episode I had been wise to have forgotten. Instead, Dr. Romero's post-hypnotic suggestion was forcing me, utterly against my will, to relive it.

8

How I endured a childhood crisis

How unfortunate that one of my earliest memories in life was as a five-year-old, crying at the dinner table, flanked by my parents, shouting at each other, arguing about what to do about me and my so-called problem.

No matter how perfect someone's life might appear, it could never be entirely free of obstacles or setbacks. In some sense, those special moments when we noticed that everything magically seemed to be perfect were precisely those which served to amplify how imperfect life truly was; as one might glide serenely across the perfection of a smooth stretch in life, which could last for months or years, it would only make more noticeable, and therefore harder to accept, the bumps one was destined to encounter in life's meandering road.

"But, Angela, the boy's got a problem that requires professional help," Dad yelled, obviously hoping his wife would agree with his assessment.

Mom looked with adoring eyes at me, raised her arm, and cradled my head in her hand. "He has the face of an angel," she observed. "You can't deny that."

"Even the Devil started out as an angel."

"Joe! Don't say things like that in front of the boy." Her hand had moved from the back of my head and was caressing my cheek. Dad glared with irritation, probably sensing that Mom's overt affection toward me made him look like the bad guy and undermined his authority.

As Mom retracted her hand, Dad seemed relieved and continued his lecturing tone. "This is what Alma is trained to handle. I'm going to call her right now." Mom nodded and let out a resigned sigh. Dad opened his new flip phone and pressed a key, presumably to speed-dial Auntie. With the sound of Matt and Emily playing in the next room, oblivious to what was happening to me, I sat quietly at the table, waiting for the appropriate time to speak.

"Alma? It's me," said Dad. Of course, she would recognize the sound of her own brother's voice, but in any case, Dad's uniquely pitched voice was easily recognizable. "Trevor's still doing it. We've tried everything. You promised as a last resort that you or someone at the clinic would see him. Well, that's where we are now. We need your help."

The problem of mine being referenced—what I had done to exasperate my folks to their wits' end—was, as the buried memory of it flooded back to me, none other than bedwetting. *Had I always had a bladder issue?* I wondered.

The phone conversation went on for some time, but when Dad finally closed his flip phone, the snapping sound it made punctuated the stillness at the table.

The decision had been made: In the morning, I would be visiting Auntie in her professional capacity at the clinic where she worked.

I knew it was for the best. Nonetheless, I couldn't help feeling sad about the situation. "I'm sorry," I muttered, almost inaudibly. I began sobbing but have no memory of being comforted or being told it would be all right. It was one of those moments when a person feels disembodied, as if one were a mere passive spectator as opposed to an active participant in one's own life.

The next day, when I got out of bed, I heard Dad's voice in the distance, which meant he hadn't already left for work at the usual time. I looked at my bed—or as I had come to feel about it, the scene of the crime. It was dry, but as if to compensate, tears welled up in my eyes at the thought of what I might have discovered. Mattress dry, cheeks wet—the same cheeks Mom had caressed twelve hours earlier, back when I was an angel-faced innocent.

After breakfast, Dad drove me straight to the clinic. Nothing I saw there—not the street, not the crumbling building, not even the sterile lobby—registered sufficiently in my brain that day which would enable me later to recognize it as an adult. As I walked meekly in the shadow of the imposing father figure that towered over me, I followed as we made our way toward a door with gold lettering which read "Dr. Gustav Romero, M.D., Psy.D."

The imagery bubbled up from the lagoon of long-repressed memories, but I couldn't help but wonder why that name later did not ring a bell for me; it should have sounded an eardrum-rattling foghorn, and yet, I had blithely met—or rather, re-introduced myself to—Dr. Romero, unaware of our earlier association. How could that be? And how creepy was it that this same Dr. Romero was permitting me, through his post-hypnotic, taco-triggered suggestion, to relive our earlier encounter? I determined not to allow this memory to slip away from me ever again.

Dad and I entered into the waiting area, and he had me sit before he approached the receptionist. After exchanging a few words with her, he motioned for me to accompany him through the inner door to see the doctor.

Once inside the office, Dr. Romero emerged from behind his desk and walked straight toward Dad. To my everlasting confusion, they embraced each other in a vigorous hug, as if they were old friends. I might have imagined it, but I seemed to notice they gave each other a quick peck of a kiss, which only further confused me. *I made a mental note during this reminiscence to ask Dad how he knew Romero and how they were so close.*

We all sat, and Dr. Romero greeted me as "Dear Trevor," as if we were already acquainted. *Could I have met him on an even earlier occasion? Since my memories prior to age five were virtually non-existent, I couldn't rule out the possibility.*

Dr. Romero asked Dad to step out into the waiting room so the therapy session could begin. As I saw Dad walking out, I couldn't help but feel that he was abandoning me. I was just a little boy; I wondered why he couldn't sit beside me while I underwent whatever treatment was in store. As I looked at Dr. Romero across the desk, I felt for the first time, but sadly not the last, that I was vulnerable and utterly at his mercy. The fact that Dad had brought me—and more so, that Mom had agreed to it—served to assure me that it would be for my own good, but inasmuch as the mind of someone at such a tender age was bound to see menace everywhere, even where none existed, I interpreted Dr. Romero's interested and focused glare toward me was at least tinged with the taint of the sinister.

Even though I thought I knew why I was there, Dr. Romero seemed less than concerned about my bedwetting. In the mind of a five-year-old, saying "I wet my bed at night" would be enough to evoke a response, but Dr. Romero's reaction was simply to say, "Oh."

The blank, emotionless expression on Dr. Romero's face terrorized me. I began to cry a bit, and whimpered, "Where's my daddy?"

"He's right outside, sweetie. Don't be afraid. I am here to help you."

"Help me? I don't want to wet my bed. It makes mommy and daddy sad."

"Then you must stop doing it. Here's how: You know it's okay to pee during the day; for all other times, you will only pee when you hear a certain phrase that we agree on. Does that make sense?"

I nodded, but honestly, I really didn't understand what I was being asked to do. One word from Dr. Romero's description stood out to me, so I asked, "Phrase?"

"Yes. Let's say when someone who is a member of the 'gurgly' says directly to you the phrase 'homey tromey,' you will relax your bladder and pee wherever you are. At all other inappropriate times, except for when you are awake, you will firmly hold your urine. In this way, your mind will overcome the urge to urinate at night, and your bed will remain as dry as a bone." Dr. Romero chuckled with self-satisfaction, at either the cleverness of his own solution or the inherently humorous image he had evoked of a bone-dry bed.

What was up with that weird word, "gurgly," and that odd phrase, "homey tromey"? The irony of it all did not escape me. I was reliving a forgotten, twenty-year-old memory, courtesy of Dr. Romero's taco-based condition- ing, and that memory itself was about Dr. Romero's ear- lier—and apparently, successful—conditioning of me to end my bedwetting.

I never did thereafter wet my bed again, but mysteriously, it was not a requirement for this solu- tion to work that I actually recall the conditioning, because Dr. Romero instructed me to banish from my mind any conscious memory of what had trans- pired during our session about it, although I was to retain its effects. He anticipated that Dad would be curious enough to later ask me about the therapy, and accordingly, he provided a soon-to-expire false memory involving dreams of swimming in an ocean. Presumably, he reckoned that Dad would accept that suppressing water-oriented dreams had alone cured the bedwetting behavior.

Dr. Romero then proceeded with some further instructions, the details of which have forever remained blurred in my mind. *I made a mental note to inquire of Dr. Romero what those instructions might have been.* Bizarrely, he followed the instructions by intoning that they were to apply retroactively. I was never clear as to how one could impart to a child the concept of retroactivity, but he must have done a bang-up job, since his mind-manipulation moment—or rather, its consequences—percolated to the top of my brain as one of my earliest memories in life.

How had this affected me in ways I could not yet fathom? Did it impact my as-yet-unformed personality? Did it form the basis for my choice of a career? Did it influence with whom I fell in love or chose to marry?

Dr. Romero's creepy face, his secretiveness, his duplicity, and his use of gibberish in his stated effort to condition a five-year-old boy made me feel like his victim. *Was I becoming his victim once more? Could I have been part of some twenty-year experiment, and if so, was the objective to control my mind?*

I had to dismiss such notions. After all, I was the one who came to him, and the fact that he was temporarily substituting for Dr. Carr was an incredible coincidence. He was not re-entering my life: I had simply stumbled back into his clutches. *Or was he instead a benefactor, who had solved my childhood problems and shielded me from the harm of my own virulent memories?*

My number was called. My tacos were ready. And so was I.

9

Shopping at the pharmacy

By the time Sunday rolled around, my nerves were frayed. The emotional impact of the taco-joint experience had been overwhelming, and the anxiety and agitation it occasioned had only grown over the subsequent days. I wasn't scheduled to see Dr. Romero again until Thursday, but it occurred to me that the prescription anti-anxiety medication he had offered might be what I needed to calm down until then.

I drove directly to the twenty-four-hour pharmacy and handed Dr. Romero's prescription to the clerk at the drop-off counter. A number of patrons were congregating near the pick-up area, and the clerk told me it would be a while before my prescription would be ready. I decided to take the opportunity first to buy some razor blades. The bank had a strict dress-code policy that required all men to be clean-shaven, so I needed some new blades before the start of the work week.

The rack for razor blade refills was expansive but surprisingly stark. In any case, the slot for my brand specifically was empty. I went to the register and asked the man if they had my brand warehoused in the back of the store.

"We're out at the moment, sir. That's a very popular brand."

"But I need them for work tomorrow."

"I realize," the register clerk said, "some folks are brand loyal, but are you sure you can't use a substitute, at least just this one time?"

"What other quality brands do you have? I don't want to nick up my face."

"If I had a face like yours, sir, I wouldn't want to, either. We're low on almost all brands, but I happen to know we're thick in stock with the Crawfordon ones."

"Crawfordon?" I asked. "Haven't heard of that one."

"Well, they're not as popular, but surely you've heard of Crawfordon blades. They're logo is the crossed swords, you know?"

"I thought those were Wilkinson's," I surmised.

The clerk looked at me quizzically. "Yeah, like I was saying, do you want any?"

"Uh, well, okay, I'll take the smallest pack, although I'm really here to pick up a prescription."

"What's your name and birthday, sir?"

"It's Trevor Crawford, July second."

"Just a moment." The clerk shuffled his feet on the rubber mat behind the counter, leafed through the prescription envelopes hanging from an overhead rod, and retrieved one. He scanned the front of the envelope and shuffled back to the counter. "Sir, you'll have to consult with the pharmacist about this prescription. Please step to the next window."

I took a few steps to the right and came face-to-face with an Asian woman in a white lab coat. The clerk was handing her the envelope before shuffling back to his register. The pharmacist asked, "Is this your prescription?"

"Yes, I think so. Is there a problem?"

"Maybe," said the pharmacist. "I don't usually second-guess a doctor, but peanut allergies are so common today, and the prescribed dose on this peanut-based medication is the highest I've ever seen. You don't have a peanut allergy, by chance, do you?"

My jaw dropped a bit, and I might have let out a telling gasp. "I have a terrible peanut allergy. Believe me, I know what anaphylactic shock is, having experienced it as a child. Oh my gosh, I'm certain I noted it on the doctor's paperwork."

"Mistakes do happen, Mr. Crawford. I'm aware that the pharmaceutical company quite recently changed its formulation for this drug, but they were supposed to have notified the physicians; I would assume your doctor is up to date on such changes. If what you're telling me is true, though, this prescription might have caused serious injury, maybe even death. Of course, I can't issue it, but I'm wondering if I should contact the police."

"Look, I don't think there's any reason to get the police involved. Let me talk to my doctor. I'm sure it was a mix-up. Whew, I'm glad you caught this, though."

The pharmacist furrowed her brow, as if rapt in thought; she flashed an expression of genuine concern but then relaxed and said, "As you wish, Mr. Crawford. I haven't had any problems with Dr. Carr's office, so don't forget to contact them as soon as possible."

I thanked her profusely and stepped away from the counter. As I pivoted to the left, I found myself next to another patron who was arguing with the clerk. Normally, there's a line for other patrons to stand behind, to afford some modicum of privacy during the prescription drop-off and pick-up exchanges, but because I was in the process of stepping away from the consultation window, I couldn't help but overhear the conversation at the counter.

"Call Dr. Simmons then," the patron barked. "That's Dr. Ben Simmons. He's at the downtown clinic."

Hearing the name Ben Simmons really got my attention. I wasn't sure why it rang a bell, but whatever bell it might have been, it was resonating in my head, loud and clear. If he were at the same clinic, perhaps I had seen his name on the directory in the lobby, when Matt and I first went to Dr. Carr's office. But it was more than recognition. I decided that maybe it would be a prudent course of action to consult with another psychiatrist. Not only was a second opinion worth pursuing, but in light of the prescription mix-up, I felt like I no longer could trust Dr. Romero unconditionally. I wondered if there was a phrase to describe changing psychotherapists. *Yeah, it's called a "brain transplant." Sometimes I cracked myself up.* The corner of my mouth hooked up into a self-satisfied smile.

The clerk killed my buzz. "Sir, please respect the privacy of other customers."

I stammered, and then it occurred to me to ask, "Sorry, but where are my razor blades?"

"Oh, right. Sorry, sir. I kept them behind the counter. Here they are. You can purchase them at the front register, if you don't mind."

I thanked him, apologized to the other patron, and took the package before striding off. I happened to glance at the razors. *Stupid clerk*, I thought. These were indeed the "Wilkinson's" blades, as I had suspected, not "Crawfordon's." *What was he thinking?*

10

Discovering Dr. Simmons

Even though it was a Sunday afternoon, I decided to swing by the clinic to verify if the name Dr. Ben Simmons was one I had seen earlier on the directory. I expected the clinic to be closed but wondered if I would be able to see the directory through the lobby's glass windows from the outside.

I peered in but found the directory to be a bit beyond the limits of my vision. Just to humor myself, I pulled on the outer door of the lobby, and to my surprise, it opened. Maybe someone was there for emergencies; the nuts seeing these doctors were apt to have mental crises at all hours on any given day, so maybe it wasn't so unusual for the clinic to be staffed on a Sunday afternoon.

While reflecting on this thought, it occurred to me that I, indeed, was one of those "nuts" frequenting the clinic. Yet, if I were judgmental about the other patients and considered them with derision, it was only because I felt I somehow didn't belong there. I had a problem which happened to be mental, but unlike the other patients, at least as I envisioned them, my problem had only recently emerged and involved acting out-of-character. I was not a disturbed individual whose long-standing bizarre behavior had come to define him. No, I was sane with a quirk, not a functional madman with deep-rooted defects.

I was standing in front of the directory, and sure enough, there shined the entry for Dr. Benjamin Simmons. *What the heck, might as well give his office a try while I'm here*, I thought. Given my experience with the lobby door moments earlier, it wasn't too much of a surprise when I found the door to Dr. Simmons' office unlocked as well. A swift twist of the handle, and I was in.

The lights were off in the waiting room, the quiet calmness of which suggested it was desolate, but the inner door to the doctor's office was partly open, and the light from inside was clearly on, as it illuminated the waiting-room floor. *Was it rude to barge unannounced into someone's office?* If the doctor were expecting a patient, perhaps my arrival would not alarm him. *Wasn't it his own fault, after all, for leaving his door open?* I was not a burglar.

As I strode across the darkened waiting room toward the light, I noticed on the counter in front of the closed reception window a cradle of business cards. I picked one and read the gold-lettered words silently to myself: "Dr. Benjamin Simmons, Ph.D., Board-certified licensed psychotherapist."

I resumed my jaunt toward the light and stopped to frame myself in the doorway. "Dr. Simmons?" I inquired, with a bit of hesitation.

The man behind the desk was balding, so as he was reading, his head was bowed down, and all I saw initially was his nearly hairless pate. As his head tilted up toward me, a stern yet comforting face emerged. He did not appear startled and asked, matter-of-factly, "Yes. May I help you?"

"Yeah, help is definitely what I need. Forgive the intrusion. My name is Crawford, Trevor Crawford." I extended a hand, grabbed his, and shook it. Then I continued, "Do you happen to know Dr. Romero?"

"Yes, indeed. How do you happen to know Dr. Romero?"

"I'm a patient of his. I've run into some issues with his treatments and am hoping to get a second opinion. Would your knowing him be a problem?"

"Now, hold on there," Dr. Simmons said. "Members of my profession must adhere to strict ethical standards. I am not in a position to second-guess another therapist, nor would I until we—that is, you and I—have established some kind of relationship. I would have to take you on as a patient before we could address your concerns. Do you want to be my patient?"

Before I answered, it occurred to me how naive I had been, thinking these doctors wouldn't stick up for one another. I decided to get a little personal, and see if I could elicit a genuine opinion, whether Dr. Simmons and Dr. Romero were friends or close colleagues. "I will be your patient if, and only if, you tell me right now what you think of Dr. Romero, both personally and professionally. There's no point in my getting a second opinion if it's bound to be the same as the original one."

"I see your point," Dr. Simmons conceded. "Okay, I will go out on a limb here, but only because I want to help you. That, after all, is why I went into this business to begin with." He paused, as if to gauge my reaction; if he wanted me to praise him for being a do-gooder, that was not going to happen: Having seen the fees they charge, these therapists were not exactly altruists. I merely nodded to him, and he continued. "Some years ago, I told Nathan—that is Dr. Carr, incidentally, who is not just a colleague, but a good friend—that this Romero fellow was not a good substitute for him. I am aware of Romero's unorthodox methods, and needless to say, I do not approve of them. He is a quack, in my opinion, if not an outright criminal."

"Criminal?" I gasped. I was not paranoid generally, but it was astonishing to hear my suspicions about Romero vindicated, particularly from the mouth of a fellow psychologist. I asked, "What has he done that's criminal?"

"I will tell you in due course, Mr. Crawford. What I need from you right now, however, is a promise to help me trap him. He deserves to be behind bars. There is a section of Hades dedicated to malevolent psychiatrists, and I have no doubt he is headed there, but in the meantime, for the sake of any future victims, he needs to be stopped before he—"

Dr. Simmons trailed off, and it was clear he did not intend to give me more information about Romero's crimes, at least not just then. After several minutes, he resumed with what seemed to be the outline of a plan.

"Because this will have to be surreptitious, we must meet after-hours or on weekends. I promise to get you whatever help I can provide, free of charge, but only after we have put this nasty Romero business behind us. I normally would not ask a patient to subject himself to malpractice, but this is the only way we can 'get' him, and I will give you the mental tools to withstand any damage he might try to inflict. Are you on board with me, Mr. Crawford?"

Working at the bank has taught me to resist rash decision making, so under normal circumstances, I would have walked out of Dr. Simmons' office without even responding. But the circumstances were far from normal, and what weighed most on my mind was that Romero had already told me he was actively blocking out the memory of our sessions. Here was Dr. Simmons, offering to help me, and maybe he was even willing to unlock whatever memories Dr. Romero had suppressed. I said, "Yes."

A huge smile formed on Dr. Simmons' face; I felt it was not simply a gleeful smile, but one tinged with a sense of relief. It made me wonder how long he had been targeting Romero and how many other patients he had approached with this take-down plan he was about to explain. Wasn't Romero merely a short-term fill-in for Dr. Carr? If so, Dr. Simmons couldn't have been acquainted with Romero for very long, unless it wasn't the first time he had served as a substitute.

Moreover, this plan seemed to require the involvement of someone who happened to be a patient of Romero's. Based on Dr. Simmons' earlier reluctance to even discuss my relationship with Romero, I gathered that Dr. Simmons was an ethical man, too ethical to have approached Romero's patients directly. Instead, I—a patient of Romero's—was voluntarily coming forward. No wonder Dr. Simmons was smiling and had become happy to see me. His giddy excitement bubbled up in his voice, as he began to explain his plan to me.

"As my patient," Dr. Simmons began, "I must warn you that you are in grave danger by continuing to allow Dr. Romero to treat you."

"Danger? What kind of danger?" I asked, without having to feign concern.

"Has he manipulated your memory yet? For example, has he put you under hypnosis and then altogether blocked your recollection of the session?"

"Why, yes. That's exactly what he did. He said it would help him deal with my subconscious mind directly. I have to say, Dr. Simmons, that it kind of bothered me. I mean, I don't like not knowing what happened for that hour."

"That is what I'm referring to when I use the word 'danger'—your mental state is completely in the hands of an individual who is decidedly unbalanced."

"Wait a minute. Are you saying he may be trying to kill me?"

"Did he assault you, Mr. Crawford?"

"No. He wrote me a prescription that contained peanut oil, and I have an extreme, and I mean deadly, peanut allergy. The pharmacist wouldn't even give it to me, it was so bad. I looked up the drug on the Internet when I got home and found out what it contained. Apparently, the ingredients—I think they call it the "formulation"—had changed recently, but allegedly, the manufacturer made every effort to notify the medical community."

"I know the antidepressant drug to which you are referring." He said both its pharmacological name and its generic or brand name, which I recognized from my search. "I recall receiving the notice."

"Well, I know for a fact that when I filled out the paperwork for Dr. Romero, I distinctly recall indicating my allergy, because it's such a big deal. The pharmacist even said it might have killed me."

"I see," said Dr. Simmons, whose countenance had evolved from one of happy excitement to that of dejected concern. He seemed to be deep in thought. His brow furrowed as he asked, "If Romero is temporarily working out of Dr. Carr's office, it is possible the notification did not actually reach him. The real question now, however, is: Should we continue? Maybe the more prudent course of action would be simply to call the police. Although, I must inform you: Our criminal justice system is highly deferential to doctors, particularly when it comes to professional judgments. I doubt such an allegation would—"

"But what about the paperwork? They'll see I wrote down my allergy, and then the creep prescribed me a high dosage of medicine with peanut oil."

"I grant that it would be regarded as a grievous mistake. But let me ask you: Was the paperwork on which you noted your allergy on a separate form, and did you handwrite it or was it a checkbox?"

"I don't exactly remember," I said. "Ha, maybe he blotted that out of my memory, too! If I try to remember, though, I think it was a separate form, and come to think of it, it probably was just a checkbox. Why is that important?"

"Well, if it were a separate form and you did not handwrite on it, then it would not be too difficult for him to substitute another copy with the box unchecked. Then it would be your word as a patient undergoing therapy against Dr. Romero's. Can you not see how that would end up in court? No, there is nothing here to take to the police."

"Okay, how about we go to the newspapers then?"

A stern look of fear and determination came over Dr. Simmons' face. Through clenched teeth, he whispered, "No, Mr. Crawford, we will not be going to the press."

I wasn't sure why my suggestion had prompted such a response. On the one hand, I could see that breaking a story like this—the headline would read something like "Shrink Gives Poison Nut to Nutty Patient"—could bring disrepute to the entire profession, so Dr. Simmons would be unlikely to participate, not to mention potential damage to his own reputation at the clinic and among other psychologists as a squealer. On the other hand, just because he was against it did not mean

I couldn't pursue it on my own. I wasn't even sure how much I could—or should—trust him. *I made a mental note to give serious consideration to taking the matter to the local newspaper: perhaps I would leave it up to them if they thought my story was newsworthy.*

"Okay, so what are we going to do, Dr. Simmons?"

"I do have a plan, but before we discuss it, Mr. Crawford, I need to find out what Dr. Romero has been up to. Let me prepare. You are not seeing him tomorrow, are you?"

"No, not until later this week: Thursday, in fact."

"Can you come back here tomorrow evening after-hours at, say, six-thirty?"

"Six-thirty tomorrow evening? Back here at this office?"

"Yes."

"Okay, Doc. I'll be here. Is there anything I need to bring, other than myself?"

"No, Mr. Crawford, but you must be willing to let me into your mind. I shall be using similar hypnosis techniques, and I need your commitment to see this through to the end. Undoubtedly, Romero has established what we call 'mental firewalls' to protect us from probing into the truth. Without your complete participation, we cannot make progress amid such psychological land mines. You must trust me implicitly."

"I trust you, Dr. Simmons." Even as I spoke the words aloud, I realized how I had already lost faith in another authority figure, namely, Dr. Romero, who had also asked me to trust him. Moreover, I had begun to lose faith in myself. The solution to the problem that initiated this whole self-discovery trip—my unexplained behavior—seemed always to recede out of reach. Despite it all, I was once again being asked to trust a new doctor, whose own motives were a mystery, and then to join in his scheme to "get" Romero, as he had described it. *When would it be time to solve my problems?* The best I could hope was that Dr. Simmons, after he satisfied his vendetta against Dr. Romero, would make good on his promise to help cure me, once and for all.

11

How I once lost Emily

For some, Mondays were a new beginning, with life neatly divided into one-week slices, but for a man who awakened every day to fresh horrors and unwanted discoveries, the days tended to blend into one long nightmare. That was the situation in which I found myself. Ever since I lost my fiancée, my beloved Bianca, my life had been nothing but a series of disappointments. Still, I had to remind myself that I was trying to get my head on straight, and once I was prepared, I would make every effort to win her back. Getting to Heaven by way of Hades: At least I had something to look forward to in the end.

My day at work was uneventful, mostly because I was on autopilot, focused on thoughts that were admittedly negative, mostly about having been a victim of Dr. Romero and the prospect of opening my mind again to another head-shrinker.

Knowing that my appointment with Dr. Simmons wasn't until six-thirty in the evening, I opted to work late, reviewing some loan documents and running some mortgage calculations. Oddly, my seventy-five minutes of unauthorized overtime were the most productive I had been all day. Plus, when all the other bank employees were leaving promptly at five o'clock, they got to see me toiling away. "Poor Trevor," they must have thought, "no girlfriend, and now he's throwing himself into his work." It couldn't hurt my budding career for others at the bank, particularly the bank manager, to have labeled me a workaholic. *I made a mental note to come in to work the following weekend to make up for my recent subpar productivity.* This little ruse presumed I would eventually have a reason to be less engrossed in my personal problems—I held out hope that such a prospect would prove to be the case, with the help of Dr. Simmons.

At six o'clock, it occurred to me that I should consider calling Dr. Simmons to make sure he hadn't forgotten about our after-hours appointment. I fumbled through my wallet to recover the business card I had picked up from his office the day before, and then I dialed the phone number. I wondered why it took so many rings, when the reason became obvious, after I found myself connected to a voice-mail system.

"You have reached Dr. Benjamin Simmons. Please leave me a message after the tone. If this is an emergency, call my paging service at—"

I immediately hung up. I had been surprised to hear that the voice was considerably different from—and much deeper than—the voice of Dr. Simmons that I had heard in person the day before. They say some people's voices sound peculiar when recorded, but this was altogether too dissimilar. *I made a mental note to ask Dr. Simmons about it first thing when I saw him.*

I drove to the clinic but parked some distance from the front door. If pressed, I could offer no reason why I had adopted such a cloak-and-dagger mentality, but arranging to meet Dr. Simmons after-hours had put me in that frame of mind. It occurred to me, though, that Dr. Romero might work late: How would I explain myself if I happened to run into him while entering the clinic? By seemingly being without a car, I could say it had broken down, and I was just going to a nearby familiar place to call a tow truck. That was a plausible story, I reckoned. Of course, those psychologists always make something out of nothing. *Why was I driving around the clinic in the first place? Was my subconscious mind at work?*

I found the lobby door to be open, but the lobby itself was eerily dark. It was reasonable to surmise that the folks working at the clinic did not exactly tend to burn the midnight oil. I'd wager that five o'clock in the afternoon occasioned something of a stampede on a daily basis, with shrinks, receptionists, and patients all making a quick exodus to their regular lives. While some people were chronically disturbed or otherwise mentally ill, from what I gathered encountering other clinic patients during the busy hours, most of them were merely neurotic, which is to say, they were mostly normal but plagued by random and unexplained impulses. That was an apt description for how I felt about myself. Neurotic people have a keen sense of the clock and know when a clinic was supposed to close. The quiet, darkened hallways were a testament to that.

In consideration of such thoughts, I came to feel it unlikely I would bump into Dr. Romero as late as six-thirty in the evening. Maybe at five-fifteen or even five-thirty, but not later. I figured Dr. Simmons was aware of the fastidious hours the clinic staff kept, which was why he arranged to meet with me as late as when he did.

Just as the previous day, I entered Dr. Simmons' waiting room, which was otherwise dark, except for the light that shone from his office. The act of walking toward a light gave me a mysterious sense of comfort, as if I were heading toward a genuine solution to my problems, or as I would phrase it, my one problem. But before he would help me, Dr. Simmons had expressed that he wanted to bag himself a fellow head-shrinker.

The door was ajar. Standing a few inches outside the doorway, I peeked into the office. As a way of announcing my arrival at the appointed time, I inquired, "Dr. Simmons?"

"Mr. Crawford, I was a bit worried you might have decided not to show up. I am very glad you did. Please have a seat." He gestured across his desk toward a large chair or settee that was situated at a right angle in front of it. I plopped myself down because I sensed he was eager to continue his greeting. He resumed, "I have thought of a clever way for us to navigate your mind without unnecessarily putting you at risk of any mental land mines Romero may have dropped."

"Oh?" I said, masking my horror at the thought of what in the Sam Hill a "mental land mine" might consist.

"Yes. The idea came to me when I was watching TV last night. I listened to some filthy-mouthed comedian that the network had to put on a seven-second delay. Well, I fail to see why we could not do the same during your therapy."

"I'm not sure I follow you, Dr. Simmons."

"Well, anything you reveal during our hypnosis sessions will go into a kind of mental buffer that will not be committed into your memory until, say, ten seconds have elapsed. That will give me the opportunity to issue a safe word, such as—oh, I do not know, something like, say, 'gamut'—and that will trigger a straight dump of the buffer without any of the information being stored."

"When you say 'dumped,' you mean I won't remember it, is that it?"

"Quite. If we hit a painful revelation that I do not feel you are ready to handle, I will simply say 'gamut,' and—poof!—it will be as if it never came up. Of course, I will keep detailed notes and can share them with you at the appropriate time."

"I have to hand it to you, Doc, that sounds pretty clever. It's almost like programming a computer. When do we start?"

"We already have, Mr. Crawford. I wanted to test it, and I have already purged ten seconds of our conversation."

"When?"

"Just now. I am sorry, but you will not be getting those ten seconds back, I am afraid. Most of my patients resist such manipulations, but you have proven to be highly suggestible, I am happy to report. Let us proceed."

I might have shuddered. If I did, I couldn't control my reaction and wasn't even sure if Dr. Simmons would have noticed it. In any case, I was very much disturbed by his admission that a chunk of our conversation had already been expunged. *And, had it been expunged solely from my memory, or had its effects on my mind been removed too?* It was an ancient adage—and one to which I have long subscribed—that an individual might just be merely the sum total of all his or her experiences. *But for those experiences to be foundational in forming who a person might be, how necessary was it for the person actually to remember them?* Still, I was not in a position to start questioning Dr. Simmons or his methods: I had to trust him, not just generally as a therapist, but I had to believe that he would make the right decisions about what I should know and when I was ready to know it. Nonetheless, I found this sort of mind manipulation terribly unnerving. I gritted my teeth and girded myself for what potentially was in store for me.

"Before we get started, Dr. Simmons, I was wondering about something. I called earlier and got your voice mail, but the recorded voice wasn't yours."

He looked a bit startled, but went on to explain, saying, "I have to do something about that. You see, I hired an actor to record my voice-mail greeting. That loud, booming voice was meant to attract new clients. I hate having to market myself. I am a psychotherapist, not a used-car salesman. But if I do not sell myself, I will lose business again. Let me give you my cell phone number instead. You can call that number day or night. I should have given it to you before."

He had picked a business card from his desk and was writing something on the back. After he laid down his pen, he handed the card to me, printed-side up; I flipped it over and noticed he had written a phone number, having underlined it twice, apparently for emphasis. My concerns allayed, I muttered, "Thanks."

"Now, back to our session. You were telling me about a childhood memory involving your cousin Emily."

"Was I?" I asked quizzically. I wondered to myself about what was going on with these disconnected episodes. Rather than make an issue of it, I decided to play along. I would pretend I knew what Dr. Simmons was talking about, and then I would make an effort to remember what that prompted him to tell me. "Oh, right. Where was I with that story?"

"You were fifteen years old, playing spin-the-bottle with some of your junior-high-school friends. You had your thirteen-year-old cousin Emily join in, and when you spun the bottle, it pointed to her. Do you recall that?"

"Yes. When Dad—I mean, my Uncle Joe—became my foster father when I was five years old, he and Mom—I mean, my Aunt Angela—really tried to make me feel like I was part of their family. Well, of course, they were family, but they wanted me to be like a son. They already had two kids, my cousins Matt and Emily, who were younger than me; we were all just a year apart in age. Anyway, Emily and I behaved like brother and sister, but I knew deep down we were cousins."

"Are you saying that knowing you were cousins changed your relationship?"

"Of course it changed our relationship. That spin-the-bottle incident was the first time I allowed myself to have romantic feelings for Emily. When I kissed her, it was the first time we kissed with our mouths, and I remember putting a lot of passion into it. She was a little hesitant, but I clasped her close to me and tilted her back a bit. I had one hand around her waist and the other hand cradling her head as I kissed her with all the feeling I could muster, just like in the movies we had seen."

"How did she respond?"

"I think when she realized how serious I was, she let her guard down, and we kissed a couple more times afterward, those times being more mutual. What was distracting were what my friends were saying at the time."

"These were your friends who were playing the game with you. They commented on your kissing your cousin?"

"Yeah. They kept whooping and hollering and saying stuff like 'Ew' or 'Gross' or words to that effect. I know some people are raised to think that first cousins are too close for that kind of intimacy, but shoot, most states let cousins marry, and it wasn't like we were planning on having kids or anything like that. I remember distinctly thinking, 'What is the big deal?' I don't believe 'kissing cousins' is much of a rarity nowadays."

"Did anyone else make a 'big deal' out of it, Mr. Crawford?"

"Funny you should say that, because when Mom and Dad found out about it, they absolutely hit the roof. Well, not so much Mom, but Dad threatened to send me away to a military academy or to boarding school. I always thought it had more to do with her being Daddy's little girl and no one would be good enough for her, and so on. Given that he had been so kind to take me in as a foster child, I can see how it could make things awkward. He and Mom had done so much to make me feel like a son, and now here I was, pawing their daughter. That was bad, I guess."

"Was that the end of it?"

"You'd think it would've been. Shoot, if hormones responded to guilt, there'd be a lot fewer people walking this earth, don't you agree?"

"Yes, but please, Mr. Crawford, do continue with your recollection."

"Sure, we were a couple of teenagers. What do you expect? We found ways to hook up without old Uncle Joe being any the wiser. We made out numerous times over a period of months, once in the girl's bathroom at school and another time, actually the last time, at night in the back seat of the family car in the garage. Something happened that I'm not too comfortable with."

"These are the kinds of mental scabs that we must tear off if we hope to heal you."

"Can't you say your magic word, Doc, and make me forget?"

"Not if the wound is to heal. Please recount the 'back seat' incident."

Before I gave Dr. Simmons the details of one of my life's embarrassing moments, I began to wonder what his motivation might have been. *Was his interest merely prurient?* I had thought we were supposed to be planning how to take down Romero. Instead, we were dredging up events from over a dozen years earlier. I kept telling myself, however, that I had to trust Dr. Simmons. I respected him and was sure he knew what he was doing. I decided to make more of an effort to suppress these hesitations and just do whatever Dr. Simmons asked me to do.

"Emily and I were, like I said, in the back seat of the sedan, really late at night, making out and doing some extra-heavy petting. We had our clothes on, but no matter how tight our jeans may have been, there always seemed to be enough slack to put a cupped hand down the front, if you know what I mean. I thought at one point with the way she closed her eyes and arched her back in a sort of uncontrollable way that we were in the throes of it, you know, but then a few moments later—I mean, like seconds later—I lost control of myself, and she totally freaked out. My guess at the time was that the "messy" result was something she neither expected nor desired, and, being an emotionally vulnerable teenager, she tended to overreact in a big way, and this was no exception. In any case, I thought her screams would pierce through the car windows, travel through the garage door, and waft up to Mom and

Dad's bedroom. And even if no one heard, I was worried Emily was about to flee the car and run into the house, screaming. I literally prayed that, if I could just make it through that night without having our tawdry encounter discovered, I would give up on sex forever."

"I am troubled, Mr. Crawford, that this experience might have adversely affected your capacity for intimacy."

"Well, of course, I had ruined my relationship with Emily, which from my perspective was really a shame, because I think I was truly in love with her."

"Did you find love again?"

"Yes, although I might have screwed that one up too. I kind of see what you mean about intimacy issues. After Emily, I did have a ton of girlfriends—quite a few even got to the stage of actually moving in with me—but none of them worked out—none, that is, until I met Bianca, my fiancée."

12

How I met Bianca

Dr. Simmons seemed eager to move off the topic of my cousin Emily and my botched attempt as a young teenager to hook up with her. Hearing me mention Bianca changed his demeanor from one of perfunctory feigned interest to one of genuine curiosity. Less inquisitive than demanding in tone, he insisted, "Tell me about your fiancée."

"I've made a career at a bank," I replied, "and it was about a year ago that I was working with an attorney on some estate matters. It involved some rich old guy named Dawson. So, anyway, one day, Dawson's daughter tags along with the attorney, something about her father wanting her to see how his business is run before she turns thirty."

"Her name is Bianca?"

"Yes. And seeing her for the first time was—how shall I say?—humbling."

"How so?"

"Look, everybody's got two eyes, a nose, and a mouth, right? But in the face of a beautiful woman, those features are, I dunno, sharper: It's as if someone sculpted the perfect face with just the right contrast and just the right symmetry and just the right proportion. When it all comes together like that, it's more than a genetic accident; it's a touch of the divine on earth."

"Tell me, Mr. Crawford, about your first encounter with Bianca Dawson."

Bank employees might often be called "paper shufflers," and I could attest to that generally being the case, although I nonetheless took umbrage at the derisiveness of the comment whenever I heard it. Papers must be shuffled, and in accordance with the laws of nature, they do not shuffle themselves, hence the need for an employee with an exceptional eye for the particular and a clenched gut that relaxed only after the final detail was satisfactorily completed. The bank needed employees, and the ones they really needed were just like me.

On that day, a year ago, I was busying myself with the task of organizing the Dawson papers at my desk in preparation for an upcoming meeting. The telephone rang. As I was so rapt in shuffling papers, it startled me. I composed myself, picked up the receiver, and calmly announced, "First National Bank, Trevor Crawford speaking, how may I assist you?"

It was Dawson's attorney calling, the man with whom I was scheduled to meet in a scant fifteen minutes. He called to confirm our appointment but also to let me know that Mr. Dawson's daughter would be accompanying him.

"Aw, that's cute," I said. "I think one of my associates has some candy."

The attorney interrupted me, "She's turning twenty-nine later this year, Crawford. The whole point is that he has always wanted her to see how his business affairs are run. By the time he himself was thirty, he had already become a titan of industry. Seems like he is grooming her to replace him someday."

"Will he be coming as well?"

"No, of course not."

"What about her husband? I would think he'd be 'grooming' his son-in-law too."

"Are you angling for a date, Crawford? As far as I know, Ms. Dawson is unattached. And before you get any ideas, I've tried going down that road, and I myself would sooner have the devil for a father-in-law, if you know what I mean. I'm probably speaking out of school here, but… Mr. Dawson is a demanding but fair boss, as I'm sure you know, but he's not exactly the nicest human being I've ever met."

The phone went silent. I sensed that the attorney regretted speaking ill of his employer but couldn't take it back. He must have been waiting for me to break the awkward silence, which I obligingly did by saying, "That's why we both work so hard to keep his business affairs in order."

He chuckled, not so much in reaction to what I said, I believe, as over the fact that I had, as a professional courtesy, covered his less-than-loyal remark with a compliment.

"Oh, one more thing about the daughter, Crawford. She's a stunner. Try not to drool over yourself during our meeting. Can you handle that?"

"Yep, can do. See you in fifteen." I hung up the phone in disbelief over how rude this attorney's last comment to me had been. There I was, being nice to him. *Did he have to respond with a put-down?* Upon re-assessing, I came to the conclusion that he was, in point of fact, some kind of jerk. What irked me most was the lack of professionalism he had displayed. I wondered why Mr. Dawson hadn't actually fired him. Running a financial empire was no small task, and Mr. Dawson always struck me as someone who demanded not just competence but excellence: *How had this attorney guy made the cut?*

And when it came to beautiful women, not to brag but, I'd had my share, and not once did I ever slobber over any of them. The heartbreak with Emily early on had propelled me into something of a desperate quest for love, a search that had me dating tons of women, quite a few of them excruciatingly beautiful, but in due time and without exception, I came to realize that the most beautiful ones were the craziest. Not only did they seem to be plagued by self-doubt, but they were invariably trying too hard to prove themselves in other areas to avoid being pigeonholed as just a pretty face. It's not that I wanted someone who was actually ugly, because that circumstance probably came with its own unique issues, but I had reached the point where physical attractiveness was no longer the allure for me that it had been or apparently was for most other men.

As I was sitting at my desk, taking pride in myself for not being as shallow as the average man in our society, in walked Dawson's attorney, heading straight for my desk, and in tow behind him was the most gorgeous woman I had ever seen. Her stride exhibited a gazelle-like grace, and as she looked around the bank, there was a deer-like innocence in her gaze. Despite the animal metaphors galloping through my brain, it would soon become clear who was the hunter and who was the prey, for upon first sight, this woman had shot an arrow through my heart, and I was quite ready to offer myself up to be gutted.

"Crawford," Dawson's attorney announced, "allow me to introduce you to Bianca Dawson." I stood but realized that my knees were quivering; I thrust out my hand toward her to engage her in a handshake and muttered, "I'm very pleased to make your acquaintance." As the words came out, I found myself relieved that I hadn't said anything I would later consider stupid, impolite, or inappropriate. I forced an awkward smile, as her soft hand brushed against mine in what felt like a caress.

"Enchanted," she said, a word I would utterly have expected from a woman of her high pedigree and sophistication. Her father was likely the wealthiest client of the bank, and it occurred to me at that moment that the attorney's earlier admonition was apt: A man would have to exert some effort over his salivary gland not to drool inadvertently when meeting such a vision of ideal womanhood.

She smiled back at me. The little hook in the corner of her mouth that formed her beaming smile seemed to mirror in perfect symmetry both the friendly crease in her eyelid and the devilish arch of her eyebrow. Her expression was unmistakable: *I can be very nice, but I also know how to be naughty.*

As I made a study of her face, I secretly hoped to find an imperfection. Then I would be able to dismiss my initial infatuation and declare her to be just another woman, not atypical of the women I met on an everyday basis. But I found nothing that would allow me to dislodge Cupid's arrow from my heart. Oh sure, some might think her features were a bit masculine, like the high forehead and wide Romanesque nose. To me, these attributes served to make her appearance all the more distinctive and indelible. If we weren't actually destined to be together, I was darn well going to spend the rest of my life trying to prove to her that we were.

The demureness of her one-word greeting resonated in my ears, while a slight breeze from the bank's air conditioner wafted the scent of her perfume into my nose. These were the kinds of sensory experiences that tended to make one want to close one's eyes to savor the moment, but to have done so at that precise instant would ironically have robbed me of soaking in the vision of her.

The stern voice of Dawson's attorney brought me swiftly back to earth when he asked, "Are all the papers ready?" I noticed that the two of them had already sat in the guest chairs facing my desk, while I had remained standing and feeling awkward.

"Yes, of course," I assured him. I grabbed the top folder on my desk to offer it to him for his perusal while I hurriedly took my seat.

He opened the folder and skimmed each document I had prepared, transitioning from one to the next with a shuffling snap. I could have taken the opportunity to continue ogling the angel sitting next to him but decided to reassert my professionalism and try to read from his facial expressions whether the portfolio I had prepared was to his specifications. His nearly imperceptible nodding at various times confirmed tacitly it was; I smiled, perhaps even smirked, at the thought that I had, as usual, done a good job.

At one point, he whispered something under his breath that got her attention, and she looked over at the document he was reading. She really seemed to be concentrating, as evidenced by her focused gaze and furrowed brow. *Oh, Bianca*, I thought, *once we're together, I will make sure you never have to worry about anything.* After I remembered that she was from a privileged background, I realized the absurdity of my little, unvoiced pledge. She hardly needed any protection, least of all from someone like me, but without even knowing it, she had brought out my inner warrior: *I would guard her from any danger I could.*

"Excellent work here, Crawford," he finally said. "You've really outdone yourself. I wish I had time to go over these documents with Ms. Dawson, but unfortunately, her father has me jetting off to Zurich later this evening."

I thanked him for his compliment and paused ever so slightly before seizing the opportunity he had laid at my feet. I countered, "Well, in that case, I wouldn't mind reviewing the portfolio with her. As the one who prepared it, I think I'm more than qualified to explain its intricacies."

"That's very kind of you, Mr. Crawford"—*oh, now it's MISTER Crawford?*— "but I'm aware the bank is closing soon, and I couldn't ask you to tutor Ms. Dawson on your own time." I cringed inwardly. I wondered if he had any idea just how many hours of unpaid over-time I had worked already on the folder he was holding in his hand or how often VIP customers such as his boss expected access, twenty-four seven, to the bank's resources, including the drudgery of analysts like me. *Maybe he was on to me; perhaps he regretted giving me the opportunity.*

I turned to look at Bianca and asked, "Are you hungry?"

"Famished," she growled.

The brevity of Bianca's reply made me realize that, since meeting her, she had said all of two words to me: "Enchanted," and "Famished." I was sitting there, day-dreaming about how many children we were going to have together, and it was all based on a smile and two words. *Kismet*, I thought.

"Me, too," I added. "The bank doesn't pay me to eat, so unless there's a problem, I wouldn't mind going over the papers with you over dinner." I looked at the attor-ney and added, "…if that's all right with you."

He was one of the ones who could arch one of his eyebrows independently of the other, and on this occasion, he did precisely that. "Very well then," he said, as he rose to give me a departing handshake.

And that was how I met my one true love, Bianca Dawson.

❧

"I heard your description, Mr. Crawford," Dr. Simmons said, "but I am unclear on why you believed Bianca was the 'one' for you."

"Was? She still is, Doc. I need to get her back. That's why I went to a 'shrink'—I mean, psychologist—in the first place. How in Heaven's name I got hooked up with Dr. Romero again, after having forgotten him for twenty years, I have no idea. Why are we spending so much time on Bianca? She's the one, I'm telling you. I don't need your help with that. Let's move on."

"Patience, Mr. Crawford. I'm formulating a theory that your attraction to your Bianca may have been due to a conditioning, much in the same way that reliving that forgotten memory was triggered by, as you say, the word 'taco.'"

"Now, wait a minute. Are you saying I'm not really in love with Bianca? Because if that is what you're saying, Doc, then you can cram your theory down your own blasted throat. Maybe we're done here." I stood but stopped short of actually leaving. I was furious at Simmons' insinuation, but, intellectually, I wanted to hear more about why he was thinking that the love I felt for Bianca was somehow manufactured. *There's nothing fake about me or my feelings*, I thought.

"Please," he implored. I obliged by retaking my seat. "In Romero, we're dealing with a twisted individual. His manipulation of your mind, starting in childhood for Pete's sake, was and remains highly unethical. I'm trying to plumb the depths that he has gone to in controlling you. I find your love-at-first-sight story to be not altogether uncommon, but given your personality, don't you find it a bit out-of-character? I mean, from a professional standpoint, I am seeing the influence of an invisible hand here."

"I can agree with you there, Doc, but I happen to think it was the hand of God, not Romero's, that was pulling the strings. I will always believe that it was fate that brought Bianca to my desk at the bank that day and into my bed that same night."

"I have little doubt you can charm the ladies, Mr. Crawford, but what I'm focusing on is why she was different than the..."—Dr. Simmons flipped back through his notepad and used his finger to read a note aloud on a specific page—"so-called 'tons of women' you dated between Emily and her." He looked at me for a response, as if he had asked a question. I just shrugged my shoulders.

"My theory," Dr. Simmons continued, "is that Romero planted the idea in your mind to date, bed, and wed, in that order, the first available rich girl who happened to walk into your bank."

"Why would Romero do that?"

"Maybe he wanted you to be happy. We are going to bring him down, on that you can rest assured, but did it ever occur to you, Mr. Crawford, that Romero's motives may have been benevolent? Let us review some history, shall we? He stopped your bedwetting, he repressed a painful memory involving your cousin Emily, and, if I am right, he indirectly hooked you up with a wealthy young woman who was not altogether unattractive. I professionally disagree with what he did to you, but can you honestly say you are really worse off for all that?"

Initially, I felt a surge of rebelliousness; I wanted to punch Simmons in the face. How could he think Romero was, as he called him, "benevolent?" I sat in silence, mulling over this idea. Against my better judgment, I began to see the situation from a different perspective. Maybe Simmons was right: An authority figure could craft a solution to a child's problems that, while unorthodox, was nonetheless in the best interests of that child. I continued to ponder the possibility.

After some hesitation, I offered, "Okay, but why wealthy? Why not make me happy with someone I had already met?"

"Maybe to help pay for the expensive therapy sessions he was engineering for you," Dr. Simmons said with a chuckle. His facial expression froze, as he realized his error of trying to make light of such a serious situation. His countenance took on a graver demeanor, as he continued, "Seriously, Mr. Crawford, we are just speculating as to his motive, so let us focus on getting you out of danger as soon as possible."

"Danger?" I asked, only half-heartedly, because although I'd be the first person to complain about the effects of mind manipulation—what Dr. Simmons kept emphasizing as "unethical" conduct for a professional therapist—I wasn't exactly afraid of the diminutive Dr. Romero, at least not physically.

"Yes. So as not to alarm you, I had considered not sharing this information with you, Mr. Crawford, but since you may presently be in danger, I must tell you that I believe Romero might have had something to do with the death of one of his patients." He seemed to pause, as if to see what kind of reaction he had evoked. I sat in silence, not for lack of emotion, but because I was stunned. He added, "That is why I am committed to bringing to an end a fellow therapist's career, once and for all."

I interjected belatedly, "Killed? How?" I knew my feeble one-word queries were making me sound ridiculous; I was trying to give Dr. Simmons some breathing room to provide me the information he seemed anxious to impart to me.

He began fidgeting, rubbing his hands and tapping one of his feet, as he gazed off into an imaginary distance beyond the walls of the therapy room. I wondered why he was having so much trouble communicating with me directly.

He finally spoke. "When one of his patients committed suicide, she had left a voice-mail message for

Dr. Romero on the clinic's main answering service." Dr. Simmons heaved a sigh and fretted, "She was going to kill herself out of a sense of guilt over a crime I later learned she had never committed."

"How do you know about this?"

"We have an on-call rotation, so the message was automatically forwarded to me as the attending therapist on duty. When I asked Romero about it prior to the coroner's inquest, he privately admitted to me that he had planted a false idea in the poor woman's mind that she had molested a child."

"And you told the police about it, right, Dr. Simmons? Somehow, I don't think you did, because if you had, Romero would be behind bars already. Instead, I'm guessing you didn't rat him out, which is why we're sitting here right now, trying to figure out how to bring down the quack."

"I have made it clear that therapists adhere to a strong ethical code. When someone, even another therapist, confesses something to us, it becomes part of their treatment, not a matter for the police, at least not immediately."

"When were you ever treating him? Oh, you just mean generally. You were trying to help him. Well, I can't say I understand why you would help him, but I'm glad you came around. Are you going to call the police about it?"

"No, I cannot. It is too late for that. But I did make Romero promise to drop his practices of bizarre post-hypnotic conditioning and the planting of false memories. At least, I thought it would cease. I took him at his word, that is, until you approached me, Mr. Crawford, with the evidence in your own encounter with him. That is why I believe we have no choice but to start building a new case against him. It is the only way we can stop him now."

"My case? I don't know about any false memories, unless he planted some. When it comes to conditioning, though, all I know of is the childhood thing. Oh, and the repressed memory he let me relive. Do you think there might be more of those floating around in my brain?"

"I am afraid that possibility is indeed very likely, Mr. Crawford."

"Can't you rip 'em out? I mean, just put me under and clear out all the triggers that Dr. Romero has planted in me, right?"

"Unfortunately, that is not quite how it works. If we know about a specific trigger—what we call a 'protocol'—we can disassociate it by reassigning a different response, including taking no action or ignoring it. But without that foreknowledge, most protocols remain cloaked."

"Cloaked? What does that mean?"

"The embedding of a protocol in the mind often—though not always—contains a directive that the subject remember nothing about the origin of the conditioning; that may be necessary for it to be effective. In other cases, cloaking is not indicated, as when the patient is trying, say, to stop smoking—in that instance, it is typically desirable that the individual retain full awareness of the conditioning."

"The triggers Romero planted in me are all 'cloaked,' is that what you're saying?"

"You are asking me to repeat myself, Mr. Crawford, and I do understand your confusion and anxiety. Let me be clear. In all likelihood, Dr. Romero has embedded numerous conditioning protocols in your subconscious, and because they are cloaked, there are only two possible outcomes. Either he himself will choose voluntarily to countermand them, or—"

"Or what?"

"Or we can neutralize them as soon as they manifest themselves in your behavior, which is what we will attempt later when we explore your psyche. But your treatment will have to take a backseat to our efforts first to oust Dr. Romero from his practice. And you will play a key role in achieving that."

"Do you have a plan, Doc?"

Dr. Simmons' eyes seemed to pivot upward and to the right as he said, "I have the beginnings of one. There are a few things I need to tidy up. When is your next scheduled session with Dr. Romero?"

"Not until Thursday."

"Meet me at this same time here tomorrow night, and we will hash out the details. Keep up the pretense that everything is normal. If my plan works, it will not only be your last session with the 'good' doctor, but it will be his last with any patient, forever."

13

Enlisting a reporter

I didn't know whether to believe Dr. Simmons' account of how Romero had driven one of his patients to suicide, but it gained some credibility as I pondered how close I had come to a one-on-one meeting with the Grim Reaper over that peanut-based medication he had negligently prescribed to me. Had it not been for an astute pharmacist being alarmed at the unusually high dosage, I would have been a character more suited to a short story than a novel.

And then there were Romero's mind manipulations. I was still astounded that he had actually treated me as a child and then blocked my memory of it, even if he did permit me the courtesy of remembering it later. *Was I supposed to thank him?* The notion of him tinkering with my brain sickened me physically.

As my thoughts careened between the suicide, the deadly prescription, and my blocked or implanted memories, I concluded that I couldn't just stand idly by, waiting for Dr. Simmons to hatch some tell-no-one plan. I wondered what would happen if such a plan failed, or worse, was never fully put into action. What I needed was a contingency plan—a "Plan B"—to ensure that Romero wasn't allowed to remain a danger to his patients, current or future.

I recalled that Dr. Simmons had, in no uncertain terms, urged against going to the press, but I felt that neither one of us was in a position to look at the Romero situation objectively. So, I decided to run my story past the local newspaper professionals and then let them assess whether it was worth their time, ink, and bandwidth.

When a town has only one newspaper, however, one would think they'd be interested in just about anything they deem newsworthy, something that would make for a bold headline in their otherwise humdrum publication. But there was usually a reason a town was small: No one particularly cared to live there. If a news organization expected to stay in business in the midst of the kind of friendly environment embracing a little hamlet like the one in which I lived, they would have to respect the townsfolk by only sensationalizing stories that involved carpet-bagging out-of-towners.

Here I was, ready to blow the whistle on one of a handful of town psychologists, who collectively would know, through their confidential sessions, more secrets about the underbelly of our fair town than any newspaper of small size could handle. The whistle I was about to blow was more like a dog whistle, and only people who really cared would ever hear it. And what did they have to care about? I'd be asking them to care about a former bed wetter—no, make that a current pants-soiler—and the horrors I had seen at the hands of a therapist while having my head examined. Any newspaper, large or small, would not be likely to run any kind of story with a background like that.

Still, I felt that I had to try. The tiny staff of a small newspaper meant there would be no gatekeeper to prevent me from seeing the head honcho right from the beginning. I walked into the newspaper building and wandered its short halls in search of the Editor's office. When I found it, I popped in without hesitation. I initially spoke with the Editor-in-Chief, a gruff-looking man who, despite his neatly barren desk, acted distracted, as if he had a million things going on. Once I got his attention, though, he patiently listened to me as I recounted enough of recent events to arouse the interest of an old newshound.

After I was done, we sat in a brief silence. He looked into the distance; the subtle fluttering of his eyes signaled to me that he was considering my story, perhaps contemplating what investigative resources he could throw at it and how the eventual headline might read. The longer he thought it over, the more encouraged I felt that I was going to gain a strong ally in the battle to bring down Romero.

He did not hold me in suspense too long, but it wasn't what I hoped for. "Let me be honest with you, Mr. Kramden—"

"It's Crawford," I meekly corrected him.

"Okay, Crawford, whatever the deuce your name is. This is a small newspaper. If it weren't for the pay-wall on our website, we'd have already shut the doors. I can't afford to waste money on penny-ante stuff like this."

I rose to my feet to leave and said dejectedly, "I'm sorry I wasted your time."

"No, wait. Hold on there, Crawford. I'm just saying, front-page banner this ain't. But I happen to have a journalist who is between assignments, and I can have her look into this Romero quack. Shoot, I'm ready for a shrink myself, so I could be a client someday: The fewer quacks to choose from, the better for me."

"Hey, is she—you did say 'she,' didn't you?—is she good?"

"Oh, the best. She was a Diogenes–Award winner."

"Was?"

"Look, now you are starting to waste my time. Do you want to work with her or not?"

"Yes. Yes, of course. Whatever you can offer. I'll take her. Thank you." My eagerness seemed to reanimate his smile. He extended his palm, and we shook hands. While he maintained his firm grip, I asked, "When can we get started?"

He finally let go of my hand to gesture toward the doorway. "Amy's office is just down the hall." I immediately interpreted it as a bad sign. Apart from skimming headlines online, I had no experience with newspapers, particularly insofar as how they were run, but I would have imagined that a star reporter would've had an office close to the editor, not down the hall from him. *Was this in actuality a brush off?* I wondered. I wanted to hope for the best.

The editor and I walked down what turned out to be a relatively short hallway, retracing one I had walked through on the way in, but the office we headed into was indeed at its end. Far from the inner sanctum of the operation, the office seemed like the last stop on the way out the door. I figured reporters spend a lot of time out in the field, so maybe I was just imagining office placement as a hierarchy. For all I knew, having an office close to the door could have been a privilege.

As we walked into the office, the editor announced, "Ahoy, thar she blows: my favorite staff reporter and blogger, Amy Bloom!" She had been staring at some papers on her desk before she fixed her gaze on him with such a glare that it demonstrated to me that this hadn't been the first time she'd had to endure her editor's feeble attempt at playful banter. The look she shot him was a mixture of annoyance and contempt. Perhaps she disliked having to answer to someone whose talents were likely inferior to her own and unworthy of her respect or subservience.

My first impression of Amy Bloom was that, like me, she seemed to be a no-nonsense type of individual, strictly professional, and someone who took pride in a job well done. I couldn't have asked for a better person to dig into Dr. Romero's background or to unearth a skeleton that would bring him down.

Her dirty-blonde hair was cropped short but just long enough to tousle when she turned her head. I had to admit that I was seeing her at a bad moment, when she was more than a little annoyed with her boss, but as she rose to her feet from behind her desk to shake my hand, a polite smile emerged from a slightly wizened yet still charmingly pretty face. I attributed the piercing quality of her cold, gray eyes to the probing, inquisitive mind I imagined all good reporters must possess.

Apart from a handshake, our introduction played out in silence, until the editor chimed in to explain that he was formally assigning her to investigate my case. As we all sat, I noticed that the two of them were leaning forward, as if hunkering down for a lengthy discussion. He relieved me from having to retell most of the details, and, although his summary exemplified a newsman's efficiency in relating facts, I thought I sensed a strain of incredulity in his voice, as if he weren't convinced that what I had told him about my experiences with Dr. Romero was true. It was the first time I realized that, in distributing a potentially libelous account, a newspaper might be exposing itself to some form of liability. *Perhaps going to the press had been an unwise move, as Dr. Simmons had advised.* Nevertheless, I imagined that star-reporter Amy Bloom would get to the bottom of it, and the editor could then decide, based on the evidence she brought to him, whether to run with the story.

After a curt "I'll leave you to it," the editor walked out, and I found myself trying to read Amy's face for any signs to indicate her assessment of the case as presented to her. I saw neither a furrowed brow of disbelief nor an avid gaze of excited interest. I was hoping for more than uninterested neutrality.

The silence made me uncomfortable, so I asked her point-blank, "Well, what do you think?" After speaking, I understood my question was far too general. The type of questions I tended to ask at work in the course of interviewing potential mortgage loan borrowers were sharply specific and designed to elicit not just solely relevant information but also every bit of data morsel someone might try to hide. In that way, my job was not all that different from Amy's: Do the research and then write a story or recommendation based on the results.

At least my all-too-general question opened the proverbial door for her. To my surprise, she announced, "I think this is a great story. Well, it could be great if it checks out." Her nose crinkled ever so slightly, which I took metaphorically, as if she were a bloodhound on the trail. I thought her unconscious gesture made her look particularly cute, and it washed away any preconceived notions I had about her being unfriendly toward me or my plight.

"I hope you're not suggesting I've exaggerated anything here," I said. "Just check on that suicide."

"Sadly, we've covered quite a few suicides, and in my experience, there's rarely a link with being under a psychiatrist's care. But I will definitely look into it." She had been typing notes into her tablet, and I could tell from the definiteness with which she pounded the screen as she spoke these words that the notes had been memorialized and saved on her device. I was confident she would uncover what she needed to turn the case into a newsworthy story.

She added, "I also plan on getting a bead on this Ben Simmons too."

"Um, I don't think you have to waste time on him. I trust him."

"Mr. Crawford—"

"Please call me 'Trevor.'"

"Okay, Trevor," she revised. I found myself enjoying the way she said my name. It sort of rolled off her tongue with a little gentle purr. I couldn't believe I was feeling attracted, even casually, to anyone other than Bianca. Perhaps my subconscious mind had resigned itself to the notion that I had lost my fiancée permanently. I shook off the idea and wondered if, at the same time, I had unconsciously tilted my head; I was aware of wanting not to appear like a nutcase, especially since, after all, I had come to her as a stranger off the street and what she knew about me amounted to little more than the fact that I was a therapy patient.

She continued, "But my approach is to follow up on every clue and see where it leads us." *Cripes,* I thought, *I really see myself in this woman*! I wondered if these thoughts were inappropriate. I made myself a deal for when the whole Romero situation was finally over: *Amy and I would be friends and, if things didn't work out with Bianca, maybe more than friends.* And part of the deal would be to put any emotions aside altogether until it was finally over.

We discussed further details and contingencies. It was Amy's suggestion that we meet a couple of times a week on a regular basis to share information. I actually looked forward to seeing her again. We shook hands once more as I prepared to depart, but this time, I appreciated the soft suppleness of her palm and the caress of her fingers against my wrist. I made a point to remind myself of my mental pledge and left Amy's office with a gallant two-finger salute that I hoped she found chivalrous.

As I walked out onto the street, the brisk evening air made me feel more alive than I had felt for several weeks, since as far back as my aborted wedding day. With that feeling came a sense of optimism, that my problems would soon be behind me. I hoped my new-found exhilaration would last for a while this time.

14

Suggesting a trap

The next afternoon at work—the middle of the workweek—it occurred to me that, my appointment with Dr. Simmons later that night notwithstanding, I would be seeing Dr. Romero in less than twenty-four hours hence. The thought filled me with dread; my pulse quickened, my stomach seemed to be gnawing itself, and I noticed that beads of sweat had begun to form across my forehead.

I took a deep breath, popped an antacid handily stowed in a desk drawer, and used a tissue to wipe my brow. I looked furtively out across the expanse of the bank, which, except for the president's office and the vault, each in their respective corners, was one giant, warehouse-like room. The transparent acrylic glass separating the tellers at the counter was buffed clear every morning so it afforded no sense of separation from the rest of the room.

My desk was situated along one wall, and from it, I could view the entire open areas of the bank. Conversely, it was like working in a fishbowl, as everyone else could also see me. I stopped looking around in order to not attract any undue attention. The last thing I wanted to do was be a nervous bank employee; that wouldn't be good for the customers or my long-term career.

I wondered about Dr. Simmons' secret plan and of what it might consist. It would have had to involve some mechanism to resist Dr. Romero's control of me, specifically the hypnosis and the memory erasures. And it would also have had to include some way for me to remember the session itself, so I could relay it back to Dr. Simmons.

During a break, I impulsively dialed Bianca's number but was immediately directed to her voicemail. I didn't leave a message—what could I say?—but I feared that she had either blocked my calls or was actively screening them. I imagined her seeing my number flashing on her phone display, the incessant blinking of which would implore her to answer my call; instead, she would mash the bypass key in disgust, saying, "Straight to voicemail, jerk!" Someday, perhaps purely out of curiosity, she would take my call, and I could plead my case. I decided, in any event, to not try calling her again until I had something of substance to say to or ask of her.

My day at work was routinely mundane, except for one event that seemed to challenge my loyalty as an employee of the bank. I had always considered myself a custodian of the bank's funds; I was not an advocate for or against the customer, but in the role I had assumed, I facilitated the selling of the bank's products to the public at large. The management of the bank routinely issued the new rates on Wednesday morning, and this time it posted a significant rise that would affect new lenders and those refinancing alike.

I had been working on a "refi" with a sweet, elderly lady and had completed the paperwork the week before. All it needed was her signature. I had asked her to come in to sign on Monday or Tuesday, but she had waited until that Wednesday so she could deposit her pension check, as was her habit. Knowing her financial situation, I was aware that the day's rate change would impose a considerable hardship on her, perhaps even to the point, from what I gathered, that she might eventually not be able to remain in her modest home. It came down to a matter of timing.

Normally, I was a stickler for these kinds of details. But in this case, I rationalized: *If the bank later foreclosed on her home, it would take a long time to sell, and even then, the bank would likely take a loss.* Enforcing the bank's rights would, in the long run, be to its own detriment, or so I told myself.

I did something I had never done before. I illegally backdated her application approval date. She was a bit doddering, so it was not difficult to convince her to sign using the same date as the approval date of the application. I later had to make up a story that I had misplaced the file to explain how it wasn't logged into the system by the end of the business day in which it had purportedly been completed. No one could doubt that this was at least a minor hit to my reputation at the bank for thoroughness and customary attention to detail. Seeing the smile on the elderly lady's face as she walked away, however, content with the outcome I had crafted for her, was enough of a reward for me personally to weather whatever consequences might accrue to me.

The rest of the workday went by briskly, and I soon found myself driving in the dark toward the clinic to visit Dr. Simmons. The eerie quiet of the vacant lobby and the long, dimly lit hallway served to remind me that our machinations to take down Romero were both clandestine and unofficial. The thought gratified me that Amy was working in parallel to investigate Romero; having someone other than Dr. Simmons involved in my case seemed at the time to be a prudent strategy.

I once again crept across Dr. Simmons' dark waiting room toward the light of his office. Whereas before, I had been uncertain and poked my head into the office before approaching him, this time, I walked straight in without hesitation.

Dr. Simmons rose from behind his desk to greet me, and as he stood, it occurred to me that, with his looming height and broad-shouldered lab coat, he cut quite an imposing authority figure. We shook hands, exchanged pleasantries, and sat to discuss the plan he had been crafting over the previous twenty-four hours.

"Mr. Crawford, I have decided that the best way for you to resist Dr. Romero's influence is for you to remain awake during his hypnosis sessions. I can accomplish this by putting you under hypnosis tonight and implanting the suggestion to surreptitiously withstand any further attempts at hypnosis."

"I figured it'd be something like that. But tell me, Doc, how can I fake going into the trance? I'm sure with Romero's experience, he'd catch on that I wasn't actually asleep."

Dr. Simmons stabbed the air with his index finger. "That will be part of my post-hypnotic suggestion. It will, indeed, involve a conscious, sleep-like state that should fool even the best-trained mesmerist."

I wasn't as sure as Dr. Simmons was about being able to pull off a trick like that. After all, I was the one going into the proverbial "lions' den," not Dr. Simmons. Even if they were defanged and declawed, lions with their ferocious roars could still be intimidating to the most courageous human. The thought of Romero somehow catching me trying to fool him frightened me.

"What do you think Dr. Romero would do," I asked, "if he caught me trying to 'fake' it?" I tried to infuse my gaze with pleading eyes, so Dr. Simmons would understand how nervous I'd be, even with his help, when tangling with Romero.

"As deranged as he may be, Dr. Romero remains a highly trained professional. I very much doubt he would ever conceive of harming you physically. Should he discover our ruse, the worst case is that we will have lost the opportunity to entrap him. Just walk out on him, Mr. Crawford."

"Okay, I see what you're saying. I don't have to stay there if I don't want to. But, that kind of raises another concern I have: What if he manages to put me under, finds out we're out to get him, and then convinces me to kill myself, like he did that other patient of his?"

Dr. Simmons' eyes fluttered, as he straightened his back and looked up toward a far corner of the ceiling, away from me. He reacted to my concern in such a startling, impulsive way that it disturbed me. I was hoping to be consoled, but instead, my concern had seemingly been contagious, and the longer he sat in silence, the more I considered calling off the whole idea of matching wits with Romero.

Without moving, he refocused his eyes on me, re-engaged our eye contact, and spoke, a syllable at a time, saying, "No. We are not going to allow that to happen."

"It's not that I don't trust you, Dr. Simmons, but frankly, you're not going to be there when all this goes down. I need more of an assurance."

"This is what we will do, Mr. Crawford: I will embed a failsafe as part of tonight's post-hypnotic suggestion." Dr. Simmons' posture had relaxed; he seemed comfortable again and once more spoke with confidence. "If you leave your session with him without a conscious memory of it, I will trigger an automatic purge. That way, it will neutralize anything he managed to get into your mind. Of course, we would lose the evidence, but your well-being must remain our top priority."

Almost as a reflex, I nodded. Dr. Simmons had promised to provide the psychological armor I needed to feel confident going into battle against a person who I had come to realize was a lifelong nemesis. Of course, I wanted nothing more than to defeat him, but if that weren't possible, at least with Dr. Simmons' failsafe, I would have both an ejection button and a parachute.

I had undertaken the task, almost like a military mission, to bring down Dr. Romero, but I had to remind myself that the goal—my measure of success in this endeavor—was not to destroy him but, rather, simply to derail his career as a psychiatrist, so he couldn't do to anyone else, least of all a child, what he had done to me.

With the potential for success looming before me, I pondered how I would handle living my life without Dr. Romero's hidden influence. These thoughts prompted me to ask Dr. Simmons directly about his end-game.

"What happens after we get him?"

"I trust you realize, Mr. Crawford, that because I will be called upon to testify about the suicide incident, I will not be in a position to continue our relationship, either as co-conspirators or as doctor and patient."

"Oh, no. I hadn't thought of that. I must say, Dr. Simmons: I really need your help to get my life back on track after this is done. Is there no way you can help me?"

"I agree that there will be a period of deprogramming that you will require, but this matter very likely may evolve into a criminal case, and, so as not to jeopardize that aspect of this affair, I can no longer see you after tonight."

"What?" I stared into his stoic face. "I can't believe this. I thought I was going to gather information that we would go over together. Wasn't that the plan?"

"No, my plan is for you to receive the incriminating information. We will then arrange to have the NPO step in to recommend that Dr. Romero's license to practice be revoked."

"The NPO: Is that the National Psychological Organization?"

"Indeed."

I remembered my earlier dealings with the NPO and how their unsatisfactory recommendations had ultimately led me to seek care from Dr. Romero. "Aren't they merely an advisory—how do you say?—uh, they have members, but they don't issue licenses, is that right?"

"I will not bore you with the details, Mr. Crawford; you are essentially correct that, technically, it is the State Board that certifies qualification, although its practice is to suspend, if not outright revoke, the licenses of any professionals who have been expelled from the governing association."

Dr. Simmons crossed his arms in what I took to be a defiant stance. I had to admit that he was the expert in such matters, and, out of a sense of abandonment, I had ended up questioning the efficacy of his plan. If he felt betrayed by my lack of faith at that point, then voicing my concern had indeed been ill-advised, but I still wasn't comfortable with the prospect of our not having an opportunity later to discuss my final encounter with Dr. Romero. I heaved a sigh of resignation and asked, "What now, Doc?"

"I shall put you under one last time. Let me now wish you the best of luck, Mr. Crawford. Godspeed."

And with that, it was like a light had been turned off. It was a sensation with which I was not unfamiliar:

I had reached a boundary of my cognition, an area of experience forbidden to my conscious recollection.

When I regained consciousness, I found myself mysteriously in my own bed, clad in my regular pajamas, the only illumination in the room being the eerie LED glow of the digits on the face of the familiar alarm clock on the nightstand next to me. The time was precisely eleven o'clock in the evening, and the bedroom hummed with a quiet stillness. I reached over the clock to the lamp behind it and switched the light on. I shook my head, as if to remove cobwebs from a vegetated brain.

Given the preciseness of the time, I figured that Dr. Simmons had removed my memory of the events that transpired just as he was getting ready to hypnotize me, lasting until the specific hour I could expect to be in bed. I would never get accustomed to such mental manipulations, whether they came from a villain like Romero or a benevolent ally like Dr. Simmons. If this was to be how Dr. Simmons utilized me, I felt it no great loss after all that I was no longer going to be seeing him.

Now all that remained was the final appointment with Dr. Romero, late the following afternoon. Dr. Simmons had fortified me with whatever defenses he deemed necessary. *But what if*, I wondered, *he hadn't thought of something?* It was the dread of the unforeseen that had convinced me that, regardless of what Dr. Simmons wanted, I should have been awake and involved at every moment of the session I had just had with him. Of course, I hadn't "just" had the session; it had been hours, but the memory lapse gave it a false sense of recency.

Being a work night, the hour was decidedly late, but it wasn't too late to call my cousin Matt for some needed moral support. Dr. Simmons might have pulled the rug out by unexpectedly withdrawing himself when I most wanted his backing, but I could always count on Matt to be there for me.

Though only a year younger than me, Matt led a very different life, one not quite so rooted in responsibility and duty as what I had chosen. He worked on-and-off, lately as a paralegal in a downtown law office, but held himself out as something of a perennial college student. That meant he could party any day of the week, and a telephone call or text at midnight wouldn't faze him a bit. If I were interrupting him, it wouldn't be his sleep; it would be his partying, which was the manifestation of his carefree attitude about life.

I managed to reach him, and he promised to come straightaway to my apartment. It appeared he was as good as his word when, after a surprisingly short delay, I heard a gentle knocking at my door. The obstructing thumb covering the peephole was one of his trademarks, so I knew it was him before I opened the door. He stood in the doorway with a sheepish grin and said, "Wassup, Bro?" I quickly let him in.

15

Preparing for Dr. Romero

As Matt entered my apartment, I shut the heavy door behind him with a thud. From both its exterior appearance and the fastidious way it was maintained throughout, it was clear that the apartment building in which I lived was secure and designed for working professionals. This was in stark contrast with where Matt lived. There, comings and goings at all hours by a parade of unsavory characters would not warrant a second glance; in contrast, in my building, a midnight visitor, even that of a close relative, could be seen as violating some unwritten rule of conduct for which I might expect a snubbing the following Sunday in the laundry room.

None of this mattered to me. I was desperate. I needed Matt's help, both emotionally and to come up with our own strategy, just in case Dr. Romero somehow outplayed Dr. Simmons in the chess match of which I had somehow become the primary pawn. I wanted a failsafe for the failsafe and was happy that Matt had come to strategize with me.

"I need to get the goods on my therapist," I said.

Matt's eyes drooped from lack of sleep, and he seemed generally groggy. He made no attempt at eye contact as he asked with a sigh, "Why?"

"Well, I've been seeing another therapist, and we both think—"

"No, Trevor, no. Can you hear how crazy you sound? When I said you needed help, what I meant was, one therapist at a time."

I tried to ignore Matt's sarcastic smirk. It became obvious that, to convince him to help me, I'd have to rehash the whole sordid situation: how I had learned that Dr. Romero had treated me as a child, that he had resorted to some heavy-duty mind manipulations, how he'd caused at least one suicide that we knew of, and that Dr. Simmons was doing everything he could to help me entrap Romero. I had to make it clear to Matt that my motivation in bringing down Romero was not only to free myself from his control but that I was afraid that future potential patients might wander into his lair.

Telling Matt that I've also got a newspaper reporter assisting me, I thought, *might make him not want to help me. So, I decided, when recounting the story, it would be better to omit that fact, at least for the time being.*

When I had finished laying out all the remaining facts, I could read in Matt's face a fierce determination; his brow wrinkled, and his sheepish expression had taken on an air of anger. His eyes twitched from side-to-side, as if he were scanning a written page, a habit I had seen him exhibit on more than one occasion when he was gathering his thoughts. The words finally came to him.

"Wow, that is some rough stuff, Bro. What a monster you've run into. Of course, I'll help, but are you sure you're up for this? Sounds dangerous."

I appreciated Matt's concern, but I explained that doing nothing carried its own perils, since I would continue to be under Romero's influence as long as he was free to practice his special brand of psychological witchcraft.

Matt continued to have misgivings, because, as he pointed out, I'd still be living with whatever mental land mines Romero had dropped into my psyche, whether I just walked away or got his license revoked. Even if Romero ended up in a prison cell, his handiwork could continue to operate on my mind unabated.

"You're right about that, Matt, but the way it's been demonstrated to me, these conditioning cues work based on triggers. Romero set one up for me to have a recollection episode when someone said the word 'taco' to me; if no one had ever said it, I'd probably never have remembered meeting Romero as a child."

As I looked into Matt's face for some glint of recognition—that he had understood the implications of what I had discovered about my aberrant behavior—I felt satisfied in my own mind that, if I could somehow avoid such triggers, I had a chance to lead a normal life again.

"You can't live like that, Trev, looking over your shoulder all the time. Who knows what triggers—is that what you call them?—that this guy has already put in your head? If—"

A look of horror washed over Matt's face, as if a dark cloud had rolled in. "What the… When you frickin' peed your pants, dude: Was that a trigger?"

"No, that's the response; the trigger is something that causes it. So, I guess that could very well explain it." I mulled over our exchange. As I pondered, I seemed to be looking into an imaginary abyss. "Criminy, Matt, good detective work. And I think I know what the trigger is, or was." My mind raced, as I feverishly pored over my memory. As vulnerable as I was feeling, being able to recall a specific fact gave me a renewed sense of control over my life.

Think, I told myself: "*When someone who is a member of the 'gurgly' says directly to you the phrase 'homey tromey,' you will relax your bladder and pee wherever you are,*" *Dr. Romero had instructed me when I was a child under his care.*

"The trigger," I declared, "is when a 'gurgly' says 'homey-tromey.'"

"You've lost it, dude. You're just babbling now. Did you take a sleeping pill or something before you called me?"

"No. Listen to me, Matt. Those are the words I heard as a five-year-old. They must stand for something that makes sense to me now as an adult. We've got to figure this out. Help me think it through. It happened at the church and then when I was on the phone with Rev. Harrington."

"Okay, well, I was lucky enough to have been around you both times and, of course, in a way, so was Rev. Harrington."

"That's it! A member of the 'gurgly'—that must be a member of the 'clergy.' Of course! And even though I wouldn't know a word like that when I was five, I sure do now."

"What about that other word?" Matt asked.

"Yeah, what would a member of the clergy say that sounds like 'homey-tromey' or something similar?"

"When I'm picturing a clergyman in my mind, the only thing I can think of that starts with the letter 'h' is 'holy.' Could that be a clue?"

"I think you may be on to something there." I wracked my brain by repeating over and over the phrase with the substitution: "Holy tromey, holy tromey…" The solution was not revealed in teasingly small steps but came to me all at once. I snapped my fingers for emphasis and shouted, "That's it!"

"What's it?"

"It all makes sense now. 'Homey tromey' must be 'holy matrimony'—that's how a five-year-old would hear it, I'd wager. And if I'm right about this, whenever a clergyman says the words 'holy matrimony' to me—"

"It's clean up on aisle six. Whoa, that is trippy. Now, I know I heard the Rev say it at the church, 'cause I was there, standing right next to you, but did he say it to you when you were talking to him over the phone, too?"

"Yes, I'm sure he did." I leaned to the side and embraced Matt in a brotherly hug. "I cannot tell you what a relief this is. I'm not nuts, after all."

"I wouldn't go that far," Matt said with a smile, as he squirmed to extricate himself from my encircling arms. "But, now what do we do?"

It had slipped my mind that we were there to strategize on taking down Romero. I had allowed myself instead to get swept up in the emotions of our discovery. *Surely*, I thought, *Bianca would finally understand that it wasn't my fault, and she'd have to take me back.* I knew there would be a time for patching things up, but the focus had to be on the matter at hand: my upcoming session with Dr. Romero later that same day.

After I brought Matt up to date with Dr. Simmons' plan to have me remain awake during the session with Romero, I asked what he thought of it.

Matt was not one to hide his true opinions. He was quick to voice his skepticism. "I don't trust this Simmons guy. He's doing the same thing to your mind as the first one. Man, these psychiatrists think they're God."

"I have to trust someone, Matt, aside from my brother." I patted him on the shoulder, and continued, "At least Dr. Simmons is trying to help me. I believe his motives are pure."

"Oh, yeah? And what about the motives of that first one? Wasn't he just helping a kid quit sleeping in a water bed? You can see they have their own—what's it called?—agenda. I say, the devil take 'em both."

"It's too late. Dr. Simmons has already implanted the triggers for a fake-awake session, not to mention the failsafe, in case it doesn't work."

Matt shook his head and muttered, "I can see I'm not going to talk you out of this, so I might as well do my part to ensure you make it out alive."

We recognized that the problem would be how to memorialize my encounter, in the event Dr. Romero successfully hypnotized me. There seemed to be no other way than somehow to figure out how to surreptitiously record the session. We discussed the additional complication that, once I was under Dr. Romero's hypnotic control, I might reveal the presence of any recording device I had brought to the meeting. It was Matt's idea for me to carry a second recording device on my person; that had the advantage of allowing me practically to volunteer the first device to settle in advance any suspicions.

But we realized that I would have to not know about that second recording device, either its mechanism or where it might be located. Matt offered to take some of my clothes to outfit one of them with a hidden bug. We agreed that I would swing by his apartment after lunch and change clothes before my session with Dr. Romero. I would not know whether the recording device was turned on at that time or was on a timer which was set to turn on in time for my scheduled meeting. For the first recording device, I would simply set my smartphone to record and save it to the Cloud; at a megabyte of audio recording per minute, the regular fifty-minute session would generate a manageably small MP3 file.

We briefly wondered if this type of spying violated any laws and if recording a criminal in the act would

nullify the wrongdoing of the manner in which we ac-
quired the information. Since a recording would serve
as its own proof, exposing Romero to the world would
result in his patient pool shriveling up, whether or not he
were incarcerated or faced a criminal charge. We took it
as our civic duty to proceed with our backup plan.

Matt and I agreed to meet later, back at my apartment at seven o'clock in the evening, to review the recordings to see if they contained anything that would
incriminate Dr. Romero or at least demonstrate his
questionable therapy methods. I already knew that
Dr. Simmons questioned those methods, and he was
well-versed in the ethical standards of the National
Psychological Organization.

By the time Matt left my apartment, it was already
two o'clock in the morning, and I found that I wasn't
able to sleep much. Not only was I nervous about seeing Dr. Romero again, but to my surprise, I was still disturbed about how Dr. Simmons had sent me home in a
daze. *Had I walked or talked like a zombie, from the time
I left his office until I awakened in my own bed?* I wondered if I had spoken to anyone, and if so, whether I had
said anything I might have later regretted. I refocused
my attention on something more positive, namely, that
we had solved the incontinence conditioning mystery.
The comfort of reflecting on that helped me grab a few
hours of sleep.

In hindsight, I probably should have called in sick
that morning. Not only had I arranged to work only a
half-day to make time for my afternoon session with

Dr. Romero, but the lack of sleep had made me a little rummy and unable to process the bank's voluminous paperwork with my usual efficiency. It occurred to me that this combination of an unproductive morning and being off in the afternoon was threatening to undermine my reputation with the bank management as a hard worker. I dismissed this worry by realizing that, unless I quickly got my mental state on a firmer footing, I was putting my career at risk anyway. The sooner Dr. Romero met his fate, the sooner I could return to my normal life as a well-regarded bank employee, a betrothed fiancée to a wonderful woman, and a man with a bright future ahead of him.

I went to work anyway and sat, parked at my desk, for most of the morning. The clock on the wall above my desk ticked incessantly, demanding my attention. The numbers on the paperwork seemed to transform themselves from familiar figures to ones of algebraic complexity. The minutes crawled by. While the time had seemed to pass slowly, when lunchtime eventually rolled around, in retrospect, the unproductive morning impressed me as having flown by. On the way out of the bank, I nodded silently to co-workers as I scampered past them, for I was once again in "mission" mode, and Dr. Romero was my target.

I drove to Matt's seedy apartment building. I climbed the one flight of stairs and couldn't help but think that, if Matt had to live in a dump, he was wise to have chosen a unit situated above the squalor and out of the immediate reach of ground-level burglars. Even in the light of midday, the hallways were dark and not without an odor reminiscent of urine or worse.

My knock at the door of Matt's apartment unit reverberated within the hallway. Hearing no motion behind the door, I sensed that, as usual, Matt was late. I didn't want to attract further attention with a second knock. The faint tapping of footsteps in the distance interrupted the silence. I was initially alarmed and girded myself for a confrontation, but as I saw Matt's face peering around the corner of the stairwell banister, I felt relieved.

Matt held his keys jangling in his hand and pushed past me to unlock the door. He ushered me into his apartment with a gesture, presumably so as not to be speaking aloud in the hallway. As soon as we were both inside, he threw the deadbolt shut with a turn of the wrist and threaded the door chain.

"Yo," he said, typical of his spartan greetings. "I have to get back to work, but I've got your spy suit ready in the closet. Hold on." He walked across the studio apartment and retrieved from the closet a single hanger holding the set of clothes I had given him earlier that morning.

I took the hanger from him and examined the outfit. I saw nothing out of the ordinary. "Should I ask?" I inquired, referring to how he had managed so expertly to conceal an eavesdropping recording device into the clothing.

"If I told you, I'd have to kill you," he said with a smile. "I'll show you when we meet back at your place at seven."

"How do I thank you?"

Matt didn't break his smile. "Thank me by nailing the jerk."

We parted with a hug, and I drove to my apartment to change clothes. Doing so invigorated me with a new sense of purpose. It was like a knight donning fresh armor before the joust. I would unhorse Romero or else die trying.

<h1 style="text-align:center">16</h1>

Recording Dr. Romero

On my way to Dr. Romero's office, I decided to check for any new calls I might have missed, and sure enough, I saw the alert for an unheard voicemail message from Amy. We had met a couple of times for coffee since our initial introduction at the newspaper. I was keeping at bay any feelings I might have had for her, at least until the Romero business was resolved, one way or another. She always epitomized the height of professionalism, both in the way she investigated every detail and in the manner with which she shared her results with me, and her voicemail was no exception.

This was only the second time she had left me such a message, and both times, I was struck by how crisply and to-the-point her voice sounded. This time, she said that she had uncovered vital information about Dr. Romero and something about his identity. I had no idea what the revelation might have been, but hearing anything about him, and especially that something about him was being called into question, fueled suspicions I had begun harboring as to whether he was even still licensed. I pondered the possibility that my efforts, having planned with both Dr. Simmons and with Matt, not to mention my upcoming ordeal with Dr. Romero himself, could be for naught. *What if*, I wondered, *he had already had his license revoked and was practicing without one?* Were that the case, I concluded, his punishment might be a simple wrist slap, as in, "Please don't treat any more patients, Dr. Romero." But I believed this to be unlikely: Dr. Carr would assuredly have vetted whoever was substituting for him during his absence.

The voicemail message ended with Amy signing off, saying we could meet for lunch, if not that day, then the next. The envelope information for the message indicated that Amy had tried calling me at around eleven o'clock in the morning, just around the time I was sitting at my desk in my unproductive, sleep-deprived stupor. I was still puzzled by how I had missed her call: I would have preferred looking into her steely gaze across a lunch table than skulking around Matt's crime-torn apartment. Of course, I had to remind myself that the change of clothes was important for the mission and that Matt's concealed recording device might prove critical to its success.

I pressed a few keys on my smartphone to add a lunch date with Amy to my calendar for the following day. The application prompted me to send an e-mail notification to her as an invitee. I had to keep my mind focused on dealing with Dr. Romero, however, so I typed a brief apology for the belated response before sending the invitation. I chuckled at myself that I was actually worried about the feelings of a woman I barely knew, while I hadn't contacted for weeks my fiancée, Bianca. I wondered if I could still legitimately call her my fiancée. I had to admit, she hadn't tried to contact me either, so until she did, I saw no reason to consider our status changed. It did occur to me that I should have checked her social media pages, and I made a mental note to do so later. If she had resisted defriending me or changing her relationship status, I would take that as a good sign that we had a chance at reconciliation. Also, it would give me a chance to ogle pictures of her beautiful face, which I longingly ached to see.

As I drove into the clinic parking lot, I made an effort to push aside, at least temporarily, any thoughts or emotions I was feeling in connection with my love life, such as it were. I had earlier established that, if I were going to be submitting myself to a mental probing, it would be better not to have any raw emotions close to the surface. Dr. Romero, and to a lesser extent Dr. Simmons, tended to poke and probe and pick naggingly at scabbed-over feelings to expose them to the sunlight, in whose healing powers psychologists seemed unwaveringly to rely.

Before exiting my vehicle, I remembered to switch on the Cloud-storage recording function on my smartphone and placed it in the outer breast pocket of my jacket, where the microphone would be better positioned to pick up conversations. I regretted that I hadn't thought in advance to test it, but I felt reasonably certain that Matt would have tested the device he had concealed. Between the two devices, I hoped to have one intelligible recording. I was also hoping the upcoming session wouldn't be too routine and that Dr. Romero would say or do something plainly incriminating.

I would venture that people behave the most unusually when trying, or perhaps willing themselves, to act normally. As I strode into Dr. Romero's waiting room, I tried, maybe too hard, to assume a casual air. Typically, I would arrive just a little early and have to wait, but as chance would have it, on this occasion, I was right on time, and the silhouette of the receptionist spookily gestured me into Dr. Romero's office without delay. Beads of perspiration had formed on the back of my neck, and rather than risk calling attention to it by wiping with a drier-but-still-damp palm, I reoriented myself so it would be out-of-view, even as I shut the office door behind me.

Dr. Romero was in his familiar position, seated behind the enormous desk that always seemed to keep us at a comfortable distance whenever we initially greeted each other. He gestured for me to take the usual seat, saying, "Mr. Crawford, I am glad you could attend what is likely to be our final session together."

"Final session?" I parroted with genuine surprise. *I knew it would be our final encounter, but how did he know it? Had Dr. Simmons tipped him off?*

"Yes, Dr. Carr has abruptly ended his sabbatical early and is expected to return this week. I was not informed in time to contact you." He lowered his gaze in my direction and said, "I apologize," but the words rang hollow.

The thought occurred to me that, if this were indeed to be the last meeting, I would urgently need to get Dr. Romero on the record, confessing his misguided methods. I had imagined the National Psychological Organization deploying their enforcement agents—jack-booted snipers, clad in camouflage—and raiding Dr. Romero's office after hearing the recording. In light of the new development, those visions, as preposterous as they were, began to fade.

I was shocked at Dr. Romero's announcement. But more than that, I surprised myself at the way it made me feel abandoned. Given that I was actively recording our conversation, on two separate devices no less, all in an effort to discredit and destroy him, the feeling of abandonment was especially inappropriate. That was always the thing about emotions, however: You felt how you felt, and it didn't have to obey any rules of logic or decorum.

The emotions infused my voice, as I stammered, "Wh-Why? Why can't we continue our sessions? I don't mind meeting you somewhere else, if that's what it takes."

"That is most kind of you to offer, Mr. Crawford, but I am afraid that it does not work that way. I am an itinerant professional; my next assignment as a substitute might be in a different city or even a different state." He held both hands out, palms down, and made a tamping-down motion with them, as if to calm me, and said, "I assure you that Dr. Carr is one of the best and can continue your treatment without much of a transition."

"You're right. I don't know what came over me. In fact, I may not require further treatment anyway. I think I may have solved my problem."

Dr. Romero stiffened his posture and in a formal tone, with unmistakable indignation in response to what I had declared, he said, "And which of your innumerable mental problems have you managed on your own to resolve?"

I sat for a while in stunned silence. Dr. Romero shifted his position in his chair in visible discomfort with the reaction in me that his snide comment had evoked. He seemed on the verge of speaking, his facial expression almost pleading to break the awkward silence, but he must have been unable to formulate the words to smooth over his jibe, as the silence continued.

Finally, I began to chuckle. When Dr. Romero joined in with his own nervous snicker, I found myself laughing, and then I said, "Good one, Doc." I paused slightly and continued, "You psychiatrists sure have a wry sense of humor."

Dr. Romero broke off laughing with me. His eyes glared as he asked, "Have you been under the care of other psychiatrists, Mr. Crawford?"

At first, I was startled, and I wondered if I had hinted at my relationship with Dr. Simmons, but it quickly occurred to me to think of the therapists I had seen before settling on Dr. Romero, and I proceeded to recount the several ones I had visited in the cross-town clinic earlier.

With his suspicions allayed, Dr. Romero flung open one of the large drawers of his desk and out of it hoisted onto the desk a contraption the size of a small desk lamp. I did not recall having seen the contraption prior to that moment, but it soon became clear that I must have been well acquainted with it, for it turned out to be the mechanism by which he induced my hypnotic trances. It was a handheld device that consisted primarily of a small, spinning wheel about five inches in diameter. Once Dr. Romero flipped a switch on its side, it began emitting a strong, pulsating strobe light, and the wheel itself appeared to spin. A pattern radiated from the center of the wheel that, when it was spun, created something of an optical illusion. After the device had powered up to what I assumed was its full strength, he said impassively, "Let us begin."

I understood the light-emitting contraption to be the mechanism by which I had been put into hypnotic trances before, but clearly, Dr. Romero had chosen to blot my memory of it, or at least of its configuration. That I could, this one time, actually perceive and be aware of the contraption and how it operated proved in my own mind that Dr. Simmons' plan to keep me lucid during the session was indeed working: Were it otherwise, I would not have been allowed to recall seeing the contraption as it appeared or be recounting later of having seen it. I took heart in the realization and felt emboldened to proceed. *No harm will come to me*, I thought.

Following what must have been Dr. Romero's regular ministrations to induce the trance, I relaxed my body and let my eyes droop to feign sleepiness. I remained mentally alert, but what concerned me was the recognition that I was unable to resist Dr. Romero's commands. My wakefulness did not hamper his control of me. My pulse quickened, and I feared both the loss of self-restraint as well as my ability to conceal my mental state.

Dr. Romero was studying my face intently. "Is there something you wish to tell me, Mr. Crawford?"

I began lifting my right arm. It might as well have been a robotic arm, for I exercised utterly no control over its motion. In fact, I tried in vain to counteract it but, even mustering all the deliberative focus that I could, failed to impede the involuntary action I was witnessing. The hand—my hand—reached into my outer jacket pocket, grasped my smartphone, and tossed it carelessly onto the desk. The glow of the large, red recording light on the smartphone's small screen drowned out even the piercing, white strobe light of the contraption, and both my and Dr. Romero's gaze were drawn to it.

Dr. Romero picked up the smartphone and began pressing a series of keys. From my vantage point, I couldn't tell what he was doing, but I surmised that he must have been stopping and erasing the recording. In a way, I felt relieved because he was far less likely to discover Matt's concealed device or even to suspect the existence of a second one.

"Is this the only time you have attempted to record our sessions, Mr. Crawford?" he demanded to know.

I was mildly troubled that, in my vulnerable condition, I would surrender Matt's device too, but two things prevented that. First, I didn't know where the device was hidden, so the idea of it remained vague to me. Second, I fixated on Dr. Romero's use of the word "you" and decided that, given Matt's indirect involvement, I could honestly answer, "No." I heard myself say the word, and Dr. Romero settled back into his chair, seemingly satisfied with my response.

"Well, in any event," he said, "I will erase your memory of our meetings, just as easily as I did this phone." I ignored his subsequent words, which he intoned in the manner of an incantation. They sounded like distant whispers. I thought of the memories this man had stolen from me, and others he might have implanted in my mind; I looked into his face, and it appeared sinister to me. I wondered if he were even aware of what he was doing or the effects of his actions. *Who better than a psychiatrist would be in a position to successfully mount an insanity defense,* I mused, *if this ever came to trial?* I looked away from him in disgust.

Dr. Romero had stopped speaking. He was not agitated by the silence that followed but seemed instead to be satisfied that his words had sunk deep into my mind, like the roots of a weed. He wasted little time before resuming.

"Since you are not going to remember this, dear Trevor, let me pose a hypothetical to you, and I would be curious to gauge your reaction." I raised my head and looked in his direction. "How devastating would it be for you to discover that you had been living a lie and that you're not who you think you are?"

"Who am I?" I asked.

"Have you no pity? I couldn't foresee what was going to happen. How was I to know that you'd try to seduce your own sister, even if you thought she was your cousin? Who does that?"

The words, despite being posed as a question, struck me like an arrow at my very core. Tears welled up in my eyes, and I hoarsely asked, "Emily is my… sister?"

Dr. Romero noticed my emotional response and said, in a more officious tone, "No. It's just a hypothetical, Trevor. My dear boy, don't worry. Nothing has happened. Calm yourself. It's all right."

His having switched to calling me by my first name—not once but twice—did not go unnoticed. *Had it been a hypothetical,* I wondered, *or was it true*? I couldn't begin to sort through the implications if it somehow turned out to be the case, so I decided right then and there to put it completely out of my mind. I assured myself that it was just another of Romero's mind bombs and that, had I been hypnotized rather than still awake, the thought would not have hurt me with quite the same devastating emotional blow as it seemed to have.

"Tell me, Trevor, what do you think of your Auntie? Hasn't she been a good mother to you? Hasn't she done everything she could for your benefit?"

"Yes. She's made many sacrifices. And I do love her, but—"

Dr. Romero was rubbing his palms together in a circular fashion, as if he were polishing them. "But what? Why can't you love her unconditionally?"

"Why did she abandon me? Don't get me wrong, I treasure my mom and dad; talk about making sacrifices: They raised me, you know. Whenever I think that my dad is really my uncle, I wonder why my mother let him foster me. What kind of mother has the heart to give up her child?"

"Blast it, Trevor, I had—" Dr. Romero was shouting but calmed himself and continued, "I mean, your mother had a career to think of."

"And do you think the Wilkinses were living on Easy Street? That ain't right, Doc."

"Joe always had everything handed to him on a silver platter: the best college, the perfect wife, and the adorable children. Poor Alma had nothing, and no one. Would you really want to see her go to the grave unloved and childless? That's where she was headed, that much I can tell you, at least until you came into her life. She needed you, Trevor, and still does. Don't abandon her now. Love her without reservation. She deserves it."

"I will," I promised, a declaration that was at once sincere and, nevertheless, voiced in the hope of putting the matter to rest.

Dr. Romero stood and walked around from behind his desk. He clasped me to his chest in a vigorous hug, saying, "I love you, Trevor, and I always will." After a pause to daub his bedewed eyes, he said, "I promise you'll never see me again." With that, he handed me my smartphone, opened the door, and began to usher me out of his office.

As he did so, he spoke some words to the effect that I should not recall the details of our session and to awaken to full consciousness once I had left the room. Dr. Romero must have thought he had succeeded in putting me into an hypnotic trance, but thanks to Dr. Simmons, I had been fortified against that, and walked out of the office already awake. I couldn't help but wonder how I had managed to fool Dr. Romero about my wakefulness; I concluded that his emotional outburst—hugging me and telling me he loved me—had clouded his professional judgment. The more I thought about it, his touching declaration had affected me too, as I felt toward him a real sense of fondness, perhaps even tenderness, however misplaced or inappropriate that might have been.

The metallic click of the closing door echoed in the otherwise muted waiting room in which I found myself standing. For several minutes, and for reasons I could not fathom, I stood there, sobbing madly, as if for a lost puppy. I had never felt so alone. I looked around, and the waiting room was deserted; behind the closed frosted window at the reception counter, no silhouette loomed. And because everything was quiet, I became aware of the sound of my own sobbing, which I managed to squelch.

Halting at every step, I ambled out the waiting-room door, down the hallway, through the familiar lobby, and to my parked car. I wiped away the tears with trembling fingers and gathered myself for the drive back to my apartment.

While winding my way through the streets during rush-hour traffic, I observed—as strange as it might be to use such a word about one's own thoughts—I no longer felt the raging animosity toward Dr. Romero that had initially prompted the mission, namely, to record our final session for anything incriminating. As terrible as Dr. Romero had been to me, I was no longer fully committed to the idea of taking him down and ending his career.

Still, I had gotten Matt involved, and he would want to know what had happened. Rather than following the original plan for me to wait around until seven o'clock, I revised my thinking, and I decided to call him as soon as I got home. He could then come over to my apartment immediately, and we could begin reviewing whatever recording, if any, he had managed to make.

Having someone else listen to the encounter I had just experienced with Dr. Romero would provide some welcomed perspective. I wanted Matt's opinion, so even if I ended up taking no further action, I would at least know what I was choosing to ignore. Matt was a straight-shooter; I could always count on him to tell me the honest truth, no matter how devastating it might be to hear.

17

Hearing the recording

As soon as I got back to my apartment, I gave Matt a call. He said he was still at work but would swing by my apartment right afterwards. Matt's job as a paralegal in the downtown law firm had been the one he'd worked at the longest, and he had even expressed some ambition of becoming an attorney someday. Whenever I considered his future, I felt like an older brother, with loving concern that he would make the right choices for his life and be happy. *Should I have involved him*, I asked myself, *in my own sordid mess*? Perhaps my experience would spare him a similar fate.

Once safely back in my apartment, and with a little time to kill, I took a look at my smartphone, the one Dr. Romero had man-handled. Of course, the recording had been deleted, with no option to recover it from the Cloud. I was curious to see if anything else were missing; I wasn't keen on a stranger poking around on my device. *Who knew where he might have dug or what information he might have extracted?* I thought. The question amused me, as I considered how for years he had been "excavating" a far more personal accessory of mine: my subconscious mind.

Other than the deleted recording, nothing appeared to be amiss with the smartphone. I checked my online calendar and noticed that Amy had accepted my lunch invitation for the next day. She had even put a winking emoticon in her reply. *Was she*, I speculated, *reciprocating my interest*? Considering how rigidly professional she had always carried and presented herself in my presence—to the point of being, one might even say, aloof—the personal touch seemed strangely out-of-character for her.

I realized that I knew next to nothing about Amy. In fact, she was working my case only because her editor had introduced us. I recalled that she could not have been basking in the light of his favor, given how he had greeted her and the remoteness of the office she occupied. Yet, he had said she was a Diogenes–Award recipient, emphasis on the word "was," which I had immediately thought rather odd. It was high time I did a little research on Ms. Amy Bloom, one of the few people I still trusted.

After invoking an Internet search dialog on my smartphone screen, I typed Amy's full name in quotation marks, followed by the name of her newspaper, and clicked the "Search" button. The results appeared, one of which offered a visual summary; I opted to click on that one, and a "Word Cloud" appeared, with one particular word emerging in large, bold letters and standing out from all the rest: "scandal." The other result websites confirmed that, a few years earlier, the Diogenes Board had, for the first time in its history, revoked the award it had issued to her after it came to light that she had planted false stories in a journalistic series over several years.

My heart sank. It was only partly that I was losing someone I could trust, not to mention a friend and—who knew?—maybe more. What made my heart ache was realizing that she was still at it, enduring the put-downs from her boss, the snide looks of her colleagues, and the hopelessness of a still-born career. *Why*, I wondered, *was she still pounding the beat*? I decided it could only be that journalism was in her blood, and the comforting blanket of obscurity would never be enough of a life for her, even if it were possible to remain incognito.

Poor Amy, I thought. It was weird, wallowing in someone else's misery for a change. Rapt in thought, I was startled when a loud knock at the door pierced the silence of my dimly lit and serenely quiet apartment. I looked through the peephole and, seeing the thumb covering it, realized that it was Matt. I opened the door, and he entered without saying a word; once the door shut, I was the first to speak.

"How do you keep getting into this building? There's supposed to be some security here. Is that guard asleep, or what?"

Matt smiled and, looking innocent, said, "Guess I have an honest face."

"Hey, before we get down to business, I just found out that Amy—you know, our reporter friend?—is a… Well, she's a fraud."

"I thought you knew that, Bro. Auntie and I were wondering why you were so chummy with her."

"What do you mean by 'you and Auntie' were wondering? What's Auntie got to do with this?"

"Trevor, don't get upset. She just wanted to know what's going on in your life. She knows you're struggling right now, so she came to me. I told her you were getting kind of a crush on this Amy chick. And we had both heard about her. It was all over the tabloids a few years ago. You really didn't know?"

I had trouble deciding which was worse: that everyone knew about Amy except for me, or that Matt had gone to Auntie behind my back to discuss my love life. *What else had they discussed?* I wondered. Then, I chided myself for thinking ill of my family, even for a moment, because they must have simply been concerned or worried about me.

I decided to change the subject. "Well, Romero erased my smartphone, so I hope your concealed bug worked. It's all we've got."

"Oh, so he managed to… I mean, you don't remember what happened?"

"No, I remember."

"Okay," Matt said, drawing the word out to emphasize his lack of understanding. "I suppose having a recording will corroborate your testimony."

"Wow, fancy word there, 'corroborate.' You still wanna be a lawyer someday?"

"Yeah," Matt said, with sarcasm dripping from his voice, "and illegally recording someone is how I'd like to get that started. Sheesh!"

I removed my jacket and handed it to him, thinking he had hidden his recording device somewhere in its lining. He waved his hand to refuse the jacket. "I'm truly sorry I'm not one of your pretty women friends when I say this, but: 'Can you take off your pants?'"

I draped my jacket over the back of the sofa, kicked off both shoes, and, as I began removing my trousers, I mimicked Matt with a long, drawn-out "Okay." He laughed, and after I handed him the pants, I went to the bedroom to put on a fresh pair of trousers. By the time I returned to the living room, Matt had placed the pants over the jacket and was eying a tiny device in the palm of his hand. I regretted that I hadn't seen where the device had been concealed but didn't want to derail Matt's focus by asking him where he had hidden it.

"Here it is," Matt said, as he lifted his palm to display the device. "The best piece of spy equipment," he continued, "that a cheap, Internet site has to offer."

I was amazed at how intricate the miniaturized device appeared; I knew nothing of engineering, but I saw what looked to be a cog in the center, although it might have been a microphone. "It's awfully tiny. Are you sure that it's big enough to have captured a full hour of recording time?"

"Yep. I brought an adapter," Matt said, as he fished a wiry cable out of his pocket, "in case you didn't have one." I wasn't as into gadgets as Matt, so it was indeed insightful of him to have brought the adapter, since it appeared that we were very much in need of one. From what I understood, the adapter enabled us to download the audio recording files from the device onto my laptop computer.

Once I connected the device through the adapter to my laptop's auxiliary port, it recognized it and allowed me to open its lone electronic folder. There appeared to be dozens of electronic files, all but one sporting a quaint reel-to-reel audio icon, and the exception displayed a needle-and-thread icon.

"Hey," I said, pointing to the files on the screen, "there's like a hundred files here. Are these all from today?"

Matt flashed his signature you-gotta-be-kidding-me look, saying, "Duh. It's sound-activated, so it doesn't record silence. Just launch that executable: It's supposed to merge them together into a single audio file."

I assumed the single file with the different icon was the executable one to which Matt was referring. I followed his instruction, and the program prompted me to save the output as a single file onto my hard drive. I would have guessed that the application scanned the device and, based on the time-stamps of the individual files, offered intelligently to concatenate them. A thermometer-style progress bar ballooned to one-hundred percent, and once the process completed, I took the precaution of copying the resulting file—the stitched file—from my hard drive to my Cloud account. I then double-clicked the file and chose, from among the list of programs offered to handle the file, a new program that had a similar icon as the executable one. The program launched and displayed a console with a band demarcated as a dated timeline. I scrolled through the timeline and clicked where the indicated time corresponded to the approximate time of my actual appointment with Dr. Romero. I clicked the "Play" button, and we listened. The first words I heard floored me.

I was astonished to hear the voice of Dr. Simmons saying "Mr. Wilkins, I am glad you could attend what is likely to be our final session together." A sense of dread welled up inside me, and I noticed that I was beginning to tremble. With a quivering hand, I managed to click the "Pause" button.

"Oh, my gosh, Matt: Did you just hear what I heard?"

Matt's mouth was agape, and he emitted a distinct though nearly inaudible gasp. "What the...? That obviously ain't your shrink's voice. If I didn't know any better, I'd say it was—"

Matt's own voice trailed off. The expression on his face, one of arched-eyebrow surprise, if not outright fear, suggested to me that he dared not speculate about the identity of the voice we were hearing.

I took a moment to gather my own thoughts. There had to be a logical explanation. *How*, I wondered, *had Dr. Simmons voice been substituted for Dr. Romero's, and why had he used the name "Wilkins" instead of "Crawford"?* My mind percolated with ideas as to how this could have happened. I had been there, not more than a few hours earlier, and I knew that what the device had recorded was not how it actually went down. *Had someone stolen the device and somehow changed its recordings?* I told myself such a notion was preposterous, not to mention that I had no idea why Dr. Simmons would participate in such a ruse.

I was distracted by the realization that Matt had never met Dr. Simmons, so it would have been a voice he couldn't have recognized. *Why did Matt think he might recognize it?* He had also said that he knew it wasn't the voice of Romero, or as he called him, my shrink. I didn't think Matt had ever met Dr. Romero either, although I couldn't rule out the possibility that he might have encountered him, perhaps as part of a family counseling session, when I was originally being treated way back when for my childhood bedwetting. *Would Matt remember his voice after all these years? Wouldn't he be more apt to have remembered his name? And yet, he said nothing when we both went to Dr. Romero's office not so long ago.*

I had to satisfy my curiosity by asking Matt directly. "Do you know Dr. Romero's voice?"

Matt seemed surprised that I would ask. "No," he said, with a subdued chortle, "but I know that can't be him."

"I know you've never met Dr. Simmons before. For your information, that's whose voice it is. I'm just trying to figure out how it got there."

"You're right about that. I never did get to meet this second shrink of yours, this Dr. Simmons, but you said you were never going to see her again, right?"

"Her?" I asked.

"Uh, isn't Dr. Simmons a woman?"

"Why would you think that?"

"Dude, the voice we're listening to is of a middle-aged woman. If you insist that that's Dr. Simmons, naturally, I assumed she was a she."

"I am so confused right now."

"I can see that. You've got two shrinks working on you, and you're still nuts." I glared at Matt, and he said, "All right, all right. Sorry. That wasn't a nice thing to say. But I'm here to help you, Trevor, not confuse you. So, tell me: What's the problem? What are you hearing?"

"The voice I just heard on this darn bug of yours is that of Dr. Simmons; I can assure you, he doesn't sound like a middle-aged woman. If anything, he's got a deep, masculine voice. I don't know what you heard, but that's what I heard. Are you hearing something else? If so, you've got to tell me what."

"Trevor, I don't know if you're losing it, mentally, I mean, but the voice I heard is absolutely a middle-aged woman's. If it weren't so snobby sounding, all high falutin', it actually sounds like Auntie's voice to me."

It was futile for me to try to argue with Matt. Neither of us would dispute that we heard two different things, or more specifically, two different voices, and both of them were of people we knew and whose voice wasn't the one we had been expecting to hear, namely, Dr. Romero's. It was evident to me that one or both of us—that is, Matt and I—were the victim of the kind of mind manipulation I had grown accustomed to grappling with recently as a patient of the two psychiatrists.

"Can we at least agree that the voice—whoever it is—said 'Mr. Wilkins'?"

Matt nodded. "Sure."

"I know for a fact that Dr. Romero greeted me as 'Mr. Crawford.'"

"Right," Matt agreed, "the voice on the recording said 'Mr. Crawford' to you."

We went back-and-forth a few times with the same result, and rather than continue the "Who's On First" routine, I decided to break it down to its components. I challenged Matt by asking, "When the voice is speaking to someone other than me, it is saying 'Mr. Wilkins,' but when it is speaking to me, it says 'Mr. Crawford,' is that right?"

"Trevor, you need to take it easy. You're giving me the impression that those are different words: They are the same. If you can't hear that, then this might be one of those episodes where the shrink did something to you. What did you call it, 'conditioning'? Think it through. Is that even possible?"

I turned the idea over in my mind and came to see the brilliance of Matt's suggestion. If he were right that the discrepancy we were hashing out were some kind of mental conditioning, it would completely explain our lack of agreement. I proposed a formula to Matt and said, "That's brilliant. If this were conditioning, it might go something like this: When someone says 'Wilkins' to me, I hear it as 'Crawford,' but when they say it to another person, I hear it as 'Wilkins.' My name is Trevor Wilkins."

"Uh, dude, it always has been."

"If that's the case, then we might, in fact, be... brothers."

"We are brothers, man."

"No, I mean, actual, real, same-parents siblings. If my name is truly 'Wilkins' and I've been hearing it as 'Crawford' all these years, then maybe the Wilkinses didn't just foster me, but they actually did sire me. See?"

"Uh, those words you're using are the same too. You know that, right?"

"Foster and sire?"

"No, not when you say them like that. I guess when you say them about yourself, you're using the same word, but when it's not about you, they're different. Holy guacamole, Trevor, that is a trip! Weird, but kind of awesome, in a nasty sort of way."

"Come to think of it, I had a little run-in with a guy working at the pharmacy. He kept calling my Wilkinson's razor blades by the name 'Crawfordons'—now, if we're right about the name conditioning, it kind of makes sense. He was saying 'Wilkins' to me, and my ears converted it to something else."

"Not your ears, but what's between 'em."

I slumped back in my chair. I sat in wonderment over the discovery we had just made. *Was it true*, I thought, *or merely a theory*? My experience with the pharmacy guy clinched it for me: It had to be true. But I could not fathom why someone would condition another human being to forsake his own name. *How long had I been deceived? Since childhood? Was it Dr. Romero's handiwork?*

"Okay, so my name is really Wilkins. If we're truly brothers, then I can't be sure if Auntie is actually my mother. Does that make any sense?"

"Don't forget: Auntie is a Wilkins, too."

I knew that "Wilkins" was her maiden name, so I didn't quibble with Matt about that. I did then say, "And she's my mother. Say it."

"Auntie is your mother."

When Matt said these words, I focused intently on reading his lips. I even asked him to repeat it. As I heard the word "mother," I saw his jaw open only once, indicating a single syllable that looked—but didn't sound—like he was saying the word "aunt."

"Say it one more time, but substitute the word 'my' instead of 'your.'"

"I'm not a trained monkey, Trevor, but if it'll help you, here goes: Auntie is your mother and Auntie is my aunt. Got it?"

"Other than 'my' and 'your,' are those the exact same words?"

Matt exhaled a deep sigh and said, "Are you freakin' deaf? Of course they are."

I realized from that moment on that I could no longer rely on my own perceptions. What I saw and heard, maybe even touched, might not be what I thought it to be. Without warning, I felt totally isolated, as if I were in some kind of mental prison. I had been lied to since childhood; that much was clear. *But as a result, had I been living a lie ever since?* When you have lost your identity, you have truly lost everything. Then a terrible thought entered my mind. "Oh, Lord," I said. "That means Emily is my sister! Did I really put the moves on my own sister?"

"She's our sister," Matt said, emphasizing the word "our." He continued, "Besides, that's ancient history. Nothing happened. Dad set you straight about that before anything went down, so to speak. Remember? I hope you're not still feeling guilty about that. Everybody's moved on from that awful night."

I knew Matt was trying to comfort me by downplaying the incident which, ironically, I had only been permitted to remember a few days earlier by Dr. Romero. And the only way I could think to avoid feeling guilty was to follow up with Emily to make sure she was all right. People might say they've moved on, and what they really mean is that they just don't dwell on the past; but as the events since my aborted wedding to Bianca had proved to me, the subconscious mind lived its own parallel life and could dwell on whatever it wanted.

Matt was sitting next to me, our two chairs side-by-side, as we huddled over my laptop on the desk. I didn't have far to reach, but I put both arms around him and hugged him tightly. It was the first time I had embraced him as a true brother, although we had always thought of each other that way. I was overtaken with grief, and sobbed in his ear, "I'm so sorry."

He pushed me away, an action which, in my emotionally vulnerable state, I neither anticipated nor welcomed. *Was he going to abandon me too?* I worried. But his words demonstrated that my well-being was his paramount concern, as he said, "Hug me later. Right now, we need to figure out what happened to you and see if there's some way we can rescue that thick noggin of yours."

Matt was right. There'd be plenty of time for reconciliations later. To find out that one's whole life had been a lie would naturally tend to unsettle a person. I needed my life back, or maybe just to have a life I could call my own. That would not be possible as long as I was under the control of Dr. Romero, or Dr. Simmons, or whoever had laid down the mind conditioning that made me doubt my identity. It was imperative that I discover any further triggers and, for the sake of my sanity, I had to find out why someone had gone to all the trouble to do this to me.

We continued to listen to the recording without comment. Several times, Matt shrugged his shoulders and used his hands, palm-side up, to indicate what we were hearing. I could tell from the exasperated look in his face that he was convinced he was hearing Auntie's voice, even though it always sounded to my ear like Dr. Simmons' stentorian baritone. I had a hard time considering, let alone accepting, that I was conditioned to hear a voice differently than it had been recorded. If something that fundamental could be controlled by a psychiatrist, specifically one using hypnosis and conditioning, I had to be open to the idea that people's entire lives might then be an illusion and certainly, in that case, not of their own making.

When the recording concluded, Matt said, "I'm telling you, Trevor, that's Auntie's voice all the way through. I'd bet my life on it."

"No, no," I murmured, quietly at first, and then came a full-throated shout, "No, it can't be!" I felt as though two tornadoes were colliding overhead, one representing reason and logic, the other pure emotion, and I was caught in the middle of the tempest. *If I could just get my bearings*, I thought, *then I could figure it all out.* I resisted Matt's contention, because if it were true that the voice were indeed that of Auntie rather than of Dr. Romero or Dr. Simmons, something absolutely diabolical was going on, and I had no idea what it might be or what further mind-bending consequences lay in store for me.

I stood and, in an effort to calm myself, began to pace. *Isn't it possible*, I speculated, *that Auntie is an innocent victim in all this, just like me? What if she were conditioned in the same way, that when I called her my "aunt," she heard it as "mother" instead? Who else was ensnared in this deceit?*

I declared, "I'm still not convinced. And more than that, I have a lot of unanswered questions. How do we know Dr. Romero didn't mess with your mind? We were both kids when I saw him; maybe he saw you too."

"Don't make me doubt myself, Trevor. You're the one seeing two psychiatrists. I know what I'm hearing on this recording, and it's Auntie."

"According to your theory—and I have to say, it's both ridiculous and kind of brilliant, in a twisted sort of way—anything I see or hear could be completely not real but merely implanted in my mind. For all I know, you might not be real either."

Matt looked straight at me with a goofy grin. I couldn't help but smile back at him. I was sure he was thinking something like, *Who's being off-the-wall now?* We had to stick to facts and what we knew, or thought we knew.

"You've finally lost it. You are a certified nut. Because, think of it this way: Even if I'm wrong, and it's not Auntie's voice on that recording, we both agree—for different reasons—that it's not this Romero's voice, either. And that's what you were expecting: to hear Romero's voice. So, you're crazy any which way you slice it. Am I right about that?"

I continued to pace, in the hope it would help me come up with a plan. "What to do, what to do," I muttered.

"What about talking to Auntie herself? That would get to the bottom of this whole thing real quick." Matt paused. "If you need me along, I'll come with you. If not, then I can steer clear of her for a while, so you have a chance to face her alone."

"Matt, I'm not going to approach her and ask her out of the blue if she screwed up my life. I need some proof first, like verification from someone other than my little brother. Shoot, I've got a star reporter working the case. She left me a message that she had some news for me. In fact, I think she said something about someone's identity, so maybe, with any luck, it might be about who these two doctors really are. As it happens, I'm meeting her for lunch tomorrow, so I can ask her then what she's found out. Let's just cool it until then."

"Are you talking about that Bloom chick? She's a known liar. Heck, she didn't win that prize for all her lies: They took it away from her; first time in history, you know. How can you trust a single word she says?"

Despite my attempts to repress it, my desperation came through, as I said with a quivering voice, "She has no reason to lie to me, and if she has even one shred of evidence to back up this crazy theory of yours, I'll have some idea about what to do next."

18

Catching up with Amy

After Matt left, I felt more alone than ever. I saw little or no use in going to bed. I knew I wouldn't get a wink of sleep after the evening's revelations. By morning, I felt exhausted, both physically and emotionally. The man in the bathroom mirror looked haggard, his face pale and gaunt; the sunken eyes evoked no glimmer of recognition, and the movements necessary to prepare for work were deliberate and effortful. I considered calling in sick, but knowing I had a lunch date, I decided to make it into work somehow. I felt like a mindless zombie, going through the motions of an ordinary and uneventful day.

I prayed I was due for a reversal of fortune. *Maybe the day wouldn't be just mundane but would prove to be exceedingly eventful.* I had high hopes that my upcoming meeting with Amy would answer if not all then at least a lot of my questions. I plodded through the morning at work. When noontime finally rolled around, I took my leave and drove straight to the newspaper. The staff at the newspaper must have already left for lunch, since there were plenty of parking spaces available in front of the building. I took the familiar route, up the steps and around the corner to Amy's office.

The door to her office was open. I peered in and saw Amy eating a sandwich at her desk. I glanced at my watch, which showed it was only a few minutes after noon. As I tiptoed into the office to get a better view of Amy, I could tell she was in the process of finishing her sandwich.

"Hey, there," I said softly, so as not to startle her, "I thought we had a lunch date. Don't tell me you found a better prospect."

In actuality, I was wondering if she was scarfing down a sandwich in advance so as to not appear too hungry at the restaurant where I had planned to take her. I had known some women who would pull that kind of stunt, nibbling and picking at their salads in public, but having pushed down a substantial meal of their own beforehand. *Why do women do stuff like that? I wondered. Don't they realize that men and women are both human, after all?*

She raised a hand while she politely chewed her last bite. When she was done, she wiped her mouth with a napkin and said, "Sorry about that. Bearer of bad news. I've got some information for you, and I'm guessing that after you hear it, you're not gonna want to stick around, let alone sit with me through a nice, little lunch in the Tea Room."

"Amy, I don't know if the feeling is mutual, but I've really come to like you as a person. I enjoy spending time with you." I gazed into Amy's eyes and was disappointed to see that her stoic facial expression had not changed in response to my amorous declaration. I pushed on, "After something I figured out last night, I doubt you can shock me so much with your news that I'll stop wanting to get to know you better. Once you're done with your investigation, I plan to ask you out to dinner, if you're all right with that."

"Mr. Crawford," she began. The aloofness of her "mister" wounded me, while hearing my old surname—knowing that she really must have been saying "Wilkins"—saddened me even further.

She continued, "You seem like a nice guy, but I'm not looking for a relationship right now." Her right eyebrow arched. "Besides, I'm sure your fiancée would appreciate if we kept our affiliation strictly professional."

What kind of idiot am I? Obviously, the dumb kind, since anyone with even a modicum of intelligence would have realized long before such a moment that you wouldn't be able to keep secrets from an award-winning reporter whom you'd asked to look into your life. I was ashamed that Amy had been brought to the point of throwing it in my face. The irony was that I feared I had already lost Bianca as my fiancée, and Amy had become a sort of backup option. In my heart, I knew that no woman wanted to be a contingency; if she weren't number one in your life, your life ain't with her.

"I apologize. I'm going through a lot these days. I hope you'll forgive me." Every woman I'd ever known has relished seeing a man beg for her forgiveness.

Amy seemed to be different, though; she acted like it didn't matter to her, one way or the other.

"No need for apology. Now, let's get down to business." She grabbed a manila folder from the top of her desk and opened it. She perused the first couple of pages before saying, "You had me focus my investigation on a Dr. Gustav Romero. You may find this very disturbing, but there's no record of a psychiatrist by that name licensed to practice in our state. Or any other state. I checked. Are you sure that was the name you were given?"

"Of course. But I told you where to find him: at Dr. Nathan Carr's office. If Dr. Carr is back, though, he's probably no longer there, since he was just substituting for him. Did you go to that office and ask them about it?"

"Dr. Carr's office is vacant, at least when I went to visit it. In my search for licensed psychiatrists, I discovered that he passed away several months ago. According to the clinic manager, the office has been unoccupied ever since. May I ask who directed you to Dr. Carr's office to begin with?"

I was taken aback that, in essence, there could never really have been a Dr. Carr, although the thought of Romero setting up shop in a vacant office seemed right in line with the whole scam he had pulled. I answered Amy by saying, "A relative of mine used to work at the clinic, so I went there, and Dr. Carr's name popped out at me. I'm not sure why I felt drawn to that name."

"Maybe that relative of yours suggested him in passing, and you don't remember it."

"No, but she did say something that I do remember which, at the time, seemed really kind of weird. She said I originally needed psychological help as a child after seeing some cartoons. It's crazy; I have no idea what she meant by that."

"It may be very important, Mr. Crawford; try to remember the exact words."

"I think I remember that she said I needed help after I had seen eight cartoons of Bugs Bunny or something like that. Can you make any sense of it?"

"You say she said 'seen eight cartoons,' is that right?" I nodded. "'Seen eight cartoons,' 'seen eight cartoons,'" she repeated aloud, varying the speed and emphasis of each enunciation. "To my ear, it almost sounds like she was saying 'See Nate Carr'—in fact, that's exactly what it sounds like."

"Wow," I said, drawing out the word in awe. "You're more of a detective than a reporter. Do you realize you've just made sense out of nonsense? I couldn't understand it, but it makes sense now. Yes, she must have been, like, subliminally telling me to go to Dr. Carr's office. Amy, you're a genius."

"No, I just listen carefully. You might try it sometime." Seeing Amy's annoyance, I sensed I might have offended her. I realized, on further reflection, that telling her she was more of a detective than a reporter came off as a backhanded compliment: She was indeed a reporter, and a very good one. *Should I apologize, or let it go*? I decided to remain silent and regret what I had blurted out rather than draw attention to it by openly apologizing.

"Okay, so this relative of mine—"

"Stop right there. Who is this relative? She's obviously in cahoots with whoever is at the center of this case. I wish you had told me about this earlier."

"Her name is Alma. Alma Crawford. At least, that's what I think she's called. For as long as I can remember, I thought she was my mother. Recently, I found out she's actually my aunt."

Amy squinted and tilted her head. "She was your mother and now she's still your aunt. What changed?"

It became apparent to me that I was getting involved in yet another word game, as I had with Matt the night before, where I was saying what I thought were different words but which came out as the same word. I loathed that my mind was under someone else's control and that it contorted my perceptions, as well as my intentions. I decided not to try to explain it to Amy. Rehashing what I already knew would be pointless; it was time to pick her brain for new information.

"Never mind. What I really want to know is what you may have found out about Dr. Simmons, if anything. And please, for the love of all that is good and holy, don't tell me his office at the clinic was vacant too."

"No. I had a chance to speak with Dr. Simmons, all right. He said he'd never heard of you. Not only that, but he also said he would never meet a patient after-hours unless it were an emergency, and in any case, he had never done so at his clinic office. Did you ever visit his office during regular hours?"

I thought for a moment. "Actually, no. But, hold on, I do recall that I called Dr. Simmons office once and heard a strange recorded voicemail greeting."

"What was strange about it?" Amy asked, with a revived interest.

"Well, maybe not strange, but rather unexpected. The greeting was a man claiming to be Dr. Simmons, but it didn't sound like him at all."

"For someone whose memory is questionable, you seem to have exceptional recall."

I ignored Amy's comment. "Well, I later asked Dr. Simmons about it, and he said something about having hired an actor to make the recording for him. I thought at the time it was kind of weird."

"Yes, that is, indeed, odd."

"Maybe it's nothing, but it does trouble me: I made a surreptitious recording of Dr. Simmons, but when I listened to it later, I didn't hear his voice, just like the voicemail greeting, which also should have been his voice but wasn't."

"Mr. Crawford, I hope you're not making illegal recordings. There's a journalistic code of ethics that prohibits us from using such information." My downcast face must have betrayed my skepticism about her remark, since I knew Amy had acted unethically herself—enough to have lost her Diogenes–Prize Award. She wisely changed subjects. "I spoke directly with Dr. Simmons and never heard his voicemail greeting. Did you ever hear that greeting again?"

"No. I figured Dr. Simmons would fix it; he said he would, I think."

"Shall we go ahead and call the voicemail now to confirm? I'll turn the phone on speaker so we can hear it together. I have his number right here."

"Okay," I said. Since it was lunchtime, I figured there was a good chance no one would be monitoring Dr. Simmons' phones, and we'd reach his voicemail.

Sure enough, the recorded greeting played and had not changed since I had last heard it. I confirmed as much to Amy, and, as she hung up the phone, she said, "That's indeed the voice of the Dr. Simmons I spoke to in person at his office, so I'd venture it's safe to say that that's him."

"No, it's not. That's the actor's voice. I'm sure of it."

"Did you say you have another recording of Dr. Simmons? Do you have it with you or can you access it from here now?"

"Yes, I can."

"Then, I might as well hear it. As the saying goes, no stone unturned. Don't tell me and I won't concern myself with how you managed to obtain it."

I put my smartphone on speaker and used it to access the audio file I had saved to my Cloud account the night before. I played just the first part so that Amy could hear my initial conversation with Dr. Romero. While it played, it sounded once more to my ear as the voice of Dr. Simmons.

Amy twitched her nose to one side as if she were puzzled and remarked, "The audio quality isn't the best, but clearly that's not the same voice as the greeting; frankly, it sounds like a woman, and an elderly woman at that."

"That's what my brother said. In fact, he's convinced it's the voice of the relative I was referring to earlier. But it sounds like Dr. Simmons' voice to me, which is as far from being a woman's voice as you can get."

"I gather you recorded this in Dr. Simmons' office without his consent, although it's puzzling that he would even mention Dr. Carr, let alone his being on sabbatical."

"No, that's what has me flummoxed. This is a recording of Dr. Romero. It just sounds like Dr. Simmons to me. And from what you said, I guess I'm the only one who hears it that way."

"Okay, so what does all this mean?" she asked, as if rhetorically. "Let's see if I have this straight. Your female relative sends you to Dr. Carr's old office, you encounter a non-existent, male doctor—Dr. Romero—and also someone claiming, perhaps falsely, to be Dr. Simmons. You secretly record Romero and on playback hear it as the voice of the fake Dr. Simmons, although others—including me, you just said—hear it distinctly instead as a woman's voice. Does that about sum it up?"

"Yep. I can tell: You're going to make sense out of this, aren't you? I'm so glad I brought this case to you, Amy. You're a really good reporter."

"Thanks, but let's put off the celebration until we figure this out." She looked past me and leveled her gaze off into the distance. "We need an explanation that matches each and every one of these facts."

"You kind of hinted that Romero and Simmons might be the same person. They look and sound completely different to me, and I've seen both several times."

"But never at the same time, right?" asked Amy. "Look, we can't rule anything out at this point. And knowing that you've been mentally conditioned, as you told me last week, and had your memories re-arranged or suppressed, possibly for years, I don't believe there's any hypothesis too bizarre for us to consider."

"Okay, you're right. Let's say Romero and Simmons, or at least the ones I met with, are somehow one and the same. How does that explain the recording? Don't forget: what I heard in person in Romero's office doesn't match what I hear on the recording."

"If I were to try to tease out a theory, I think… No, wait, that's too far-out."

"What? I thought you said nothing was off the table."

"Maybe it's not as preposterous as it may sound. Okay, I have a theory, a working theory. Care to hear it?"

"More than anything I've ever wanted to hear in my entire life."

"I think that your female relative sent you to Dr. Carr's vacant office and then she herself showed up there as Dr. Romero. She also somehow impersonated Dr. Simmons and got you to visit his office after-hours. The idea that this Simmons was helping you was just a ruse to cover her tracks. That's the 'who' of this: your relative—what did you call her, 'Alma'? She's behind it all."

"A few days ago, I would have said there's no way Auntie is even involved in this, not to mention behind it all. But, okay, let's run with it: Let's say she's the mastermind who's pulling all the strings here. You haven't explained why, when I listen to the secret recording, I keep hearing Dr. Simmons' voice."

"Fair enough. I get your question. From all you've told me, though, is it much of a stretch to say that you're not seeing or hearing things as they really are? I'll answer that: No, it's not. You're under the influence of post-hypnotic suggestion. Someone's controlling your behavior behind the scenes. Why can't that someone be Alma?"

"All right," I conceded. "Say it's her. So?"

"The voicemail greeting we heard just now when I called Dr. Simmons' office—you said you asked 'him' about it, right? If my theory is correct, you were actually asking her, by which I mean, you were asking her posing as Dr. Simmons. I can only imagine how that must have spooked her. She had to worry that you'd someday hear her voice on some recording somewhere, maybe even her own cell phone voicemail greeting, so under hypnosis, I would guess that she must have wired your brain to hear her Simmons voice whenever you heard her recorded voice. Doesn't that make sense? That's the layer she needed to keep you from knowing it was her, and it explains why you're hearing that on your recording."

"Oh, Amy, do you realize how crazy that sounds? Let's break this down. You say she is Dr. Simmons. Okay, how'd she pull that off to begin with?"

"She's Romero too, don't forget. As Romero, she invents this Simmons character based on a real doctor and fogs up your brain so that when you visit her in the other office, you see and hear her as if she were this Dr. Simmons. Are you with me so far?"

My voice and posture belied a deep skepticism. "So far, maybe."

"Then she makes you believe Simmons is helping you defeat Romero, but both of them are really her. See? The only thing I'm a bit fuzzy on is how she made sure you'd never see Romero and Simmons at the same time, especially since they were supposed to be working in the same clinic."

"Well, Dr. Romero only worked during the day, which is when I saw him, and Dr. Simmons would only see me after-hours. I did kind of think that was odd. It would certainly guarantee that I would keep 'em separate, though."

"So, I think she messed with your mind and made you see or hear someone else at various times or locations, when it was her all along. I did some extensive research for a series on the brain a couple of years ago, and I can tell you that the mind is a powerful tool, even, or maybe especially, when it's been instructed to deceive itself. That's the 'how' of it. What we need as the final piece is the 'why' of it all."

"If you're saying that Alma impersonated a male psychiatrist—no, wait, make that two male psychiatrists—she must've had some kind of motive." I tried to remember if I had told Amy everything I knew about Romero. "Hmmm. Did I ever tell you that I first met Dr. Romero when I was a child? My folks took me to see him when I was, like, five years old. Until the other day, I hadn't remembered that."

"No, you sure didn't mention it to me. Since we're speculating that Romero may not even exist, I would take it as confirmation that your Alma has been in your head since your early childhood. What led up to your initial visit with her as Romero, if I may ask?"

In our initial meeting about the case, I had felt I had no choice but to explain to Amy why I was seeing Dr. Romero, so she already knew about the wedding incident. That took away most of the embarrassment of confessing that it was childhood bedwetting that got me in Romero's clutches at the start. "What's odd, though, is that it turned out to be my earliest memory."

"That's an important clue," Amy declared. "It suggests that Alma might have exerted her control over you prior to that. It wouldn't surprise me if she conditioned your bedwetting, just to introduce you to her alter ego."

"I pieced together—well, with the help of my brother—that she's not really my mother. Oh, hold on, you're not hearing the word I'm saying; I found that out too. Let me put it this way: Alma's name is right there, squarely on my birth certificate; I've seen it with my own eyes, but it shouldn't be there. Do you understand what I'm saying?"

"I came across your birth notice. It's not something most people look up or even see themselves. I got the idea from the Birther Movement. Want to know what I found? I know for a fact that she's not mentioned at all, this Alma person. So I do understand exactly what you're saying. My guess is that your brain isn't seeing your birth certificate as it truly is: Some conditioning is making you see it with her name on it when it's really another name."

"Why would she try to convince me that… I know you're not going to hear this correctly, so I'm just saying for myself: that she was my mother?"

"I can infer what you're saying. And let me ask you, does Alma have any other children?"

"No."

"Then we may just have our 'why' in that: A childless woman persuades a boy that his parents are not his and that she's actually his mother. I once wrote of a case where a woman stole a baby from a hospital maternity ward. The mother instinct can be very strong. As I see it, this could be the one explanation that covers the facts and makes some kind of sense."

I wasn't sure whether to believe her—her facts or her reasoning—given her own scandalous history. In my mind, I had come to view Amy as not being a lot better than these psychiatrists, whether it was Alma or not. They all had "planted" false stories: Amy in the newspaper, and the doctors in my mind or into the minds of others in their care. I had come to lose faith in both these esteemed institutions, that is, journalism and mental health care.

It would have done no good to throw Amy's past into her face, especially when she had been so useful in helping me figure things out up to that point. I knew, thanks to Amy, that Auntie had sent me to Dr. Carr's office to an impostor, and from my recording, I knew Romero and Simmons were the same person. Despite my reluctance,

I had to consider it plausible that Auntie was behind it all, perhaps to make me the child she never had.

I decided to ask Amy for a little advice. "My brother thinks I should confront her, but it sounds like such a bizarre accusation that I wouldn't know what to expect from her. What do you think?"

Amy averted her gaze and, at first glance, appeared rapt in thought. After a few moments, she said, "Is your goal to send her to prison or to let this go?"

The silence resurfaced, as I tried to let Amy's question sink in. I wondered how Amy could even imagine that I might just let go of something that had probably ruined my life. "What difference does it make?"

"You might regard her actions as, well, kind of pathetic. I'm not saying you should forgive her, but you might try to understand what motivated her to do what she did. By our figuring it out, if indeed we have, then you've been freed from her influence. Maybe that's enough for you."

"I see your point," I said, as I felt, in the pit of my stomach, the awful sense of pity that Amy was suggesting might be appropriate. "But I can't go on pretending with her. You say let it go, but how do I do that?"

"Let me think," Amy said, as she seemed to be mentally mulling various options. "I think I have an idea. It would help both of you to save face."

"What?"

"May I suggest, Mr. Crawford, that you arrange to see her as Dr. Simmons one more time? Tell Simmons—or rather, her—that you found out that Dr. Romero had brainwashed you since childhood and that you now know the truth. Only, stop short of the whole truth: Let her think you're not onto her little Simmons scheme. This would allow you to tidy things up, letting her bow out gracefully without ever knowing that you know the whole story, and you both can move on from there. That's what I'd do if I were in your shoes."

"That is nothing short of brilliant, Amy. I'm going to say it again: You're some kind of genius. I only hope I can get Dr. Simmons—I mean, her—to see me once more. He said he wouldn't see me again, but if I hit him with the Romero bombshell, he—I mean, she—just might let me talk it out. Thank you so much, not only for that advice but for all you've done for me."

"I assume for the sake of your family that we'll be killing this story. It won't be the first story I started on that didn't run in this lousy paper. I'll just tell my boss it didn't pan out. Incidentally, he kinda thinks you're nuts anyway."

That editor had seemed the day I met him like he was giving me the brush-off. I decided not to take his opinion personally; ever since my wedding day, even I thought I was crazy, but I had come to realize, given my experiences and how I had miraculously survived them, that I must be, after all, one of the sanest people around.

I thanked Amy again. For all her help, I could have kissed her, and I would have done so if I believed she'd have permitted it. My rule, however, had always been to allow a girl to reject me only once a day. I opted instead for the less-amorous handshake, although I took no small enjoyment from touching her and shaking her hand a little longer than mere acquaintance should sanction. I figured it would likely be the last time our paths crossed, so I made my farewell a bit heartier.

"Goodbye, Amy. I'll never forget you or what you did for me," I muttered, as I walked out of her office, glancing back only once to see her smiling face. I had a little skip in my step as I navigated the corner of the hallway to the outside door. As I stepped out into the open air, I felt truly like a new man.

19

Confronting Dr. Simmons

The following day, my head was spinning with all the revelations that had come to light in the span of the preceding twenty-four hours. With Matt's help and Amy's investigation, I had come to realize that my own aunt had manipulated me from childhood so she could claim me as her son. My stomach churned at the thought of how pathetic it was and what elaborate lengths Auntie had gone to in order to perpetrate her sinister little scheme.

Amy had impressed on me that my best shot for some closure was to see Auntie one last time in the guise of Dr. Simmons. I knew my motivation was never about revenge; all I wanted was to make the break so I could get on with my life. My mind might have been in shambles, but I looked forward to going home and hugging my mom and dad—they really were my parents, after all—and maybe patching things up with Bianca. I just had to get through one more encounter with the so-called Dr. Simmons, and then I'd be a free man again.

I grabbed my smartphone and scrolled through the contacts. I noticed Auntie's cell phone number as I continued to scroll down to the one Dr. Simmons had given me for contacting him outside of his office. I halfheartedly hoped to see that they were the same telephone number but had no such luck. I guessed that Auntie had bought one of those disposable "burner" phones to use when she was impersonating Simmons. I surmised that she must have embedded a protocol—a term she had told me about as Simmons—that, whenever I called the given cell phone number, I would hear her voice as that of Dr. Simmons. As much as I resented being manipulated, I admired the cleverness of the ruse.

If it were a disposable "burner" phone she had used, what if she had literally disposed of it already? I had no choice but to give it a try. With the contact for Dr. Simmons highlighted, I pressed the "Send" key and waited patiently as it rang a couple of times. I was surprised that after only two rings, s/he answered, perhaps alerted by the caller ID.

It was the voice of Dr. Simmons. "Mr. Crawford, I thought I made it clear that we can no longer be in contact. Please do not call me again."

"Wait," I said, allowing the desperation to soak into my voice for fear s/he was about to hang up on me. "I need to speak to you. It's vitally important. Please, Dr. Simmons. I need your help."

"I am so sorry, but I cannot help you, Mr. Crawford."

I had to think of something that would stop him from ending the call. My mind scrambled for an excuse.

Then, it occurred to me to use a piece of information, undoubtedly false, that Dr. Simmons had once fed me; I would feed it right back to him. I said, "No, wait. I think Dr. Romero planted a suicide thought in my mind. If you don't help me, Dr. Simmons, I swear, I'll take my life the moment you abandon me. I really need to see you, as soon as possible."

Silence ensued. I sensed that my ploy might have worked and that s/he would be more accommodating. If it really were Auntie I was speaking to, she'd move mountains to protect me from ending my own life, even if those mountains ended up burying her. The reply came, "Do you believe you will be able to hold off taking any rash action, Mr. Crawford, until I have the opportunity to meet with you in person tonight at six-thirty in my office?"

I promised to resist any suicidal urges and expressed my gratitude that s/he had agreed to see me once more during my time of crisis. I clicked the "End" key and immediately began plotting how I would steer the confrontation. I went about my day, staying busy while fighting distractions, until the evening arrived, and I found myself, lurking as usual, at the door of Dr. Simmons' inner office.

A rolling gesture of his hand mutely signaled me to enter. I sank into the familiar seat and heaved an audible sigh over the prospect of what was to come. "Thank you so much, Dr. Simmons, for agreeing to see me one more time."

"I must say, Mr. Crawford, it is I who am relieved to see you. When you told me of your suicidal tendencies this morning, I should have been more professional and dropped my appointments to see you right away."

"It's okay, Doc."

"What a relief that you made it through the day. Have you had any further suicidal thoughts?"

"No. Well, about that: I might have exaggerated that a little bit. I really needed to see you about my final session with Dr. Romero. And you're the only one who can give me some closure."

"So you're not suffering from suicidal thoughts then?" In response, I shook my head. "It was wholly unexpected, especially your claim that Dr. Romero had planted the idea for it in your mind. You see, to be totally honest, I must confess, I lied to you too, but it was for a noble cause."

Oh, I thought, *is it "confession time" already? How far was this going to go?* I scoffed when I heard the phrase "noble cause," since, to my mind, it would be better described as a "selfish cause." Fortunately, my scoff had barely been audible.

Dr. Simmons continued, "There was a suicide, and I will be testifying at the inquest, but it was not one of Dr. Romero's patients. I have my own motives for wanting to broker an amicable end of your treatment with Dr. Romero, and I crudely used the suicide incident to make that happen."

"Now, wait just one minute here. I thought you wanted to bring Romero down. You said you disapproved of his methods. You lied to me?"

"Please consider my point-of-view. As a colleague of Dr. Romero's, I became aware of your—shall we say, unorthodox?—treatment, and I found myself in the middle of it. I regarded it as my ethical and professional duty to bring it to an end by allowing Dr. Romero to release you from all the protocols he may have embedded."

I glared at Dr. Simmons with a burning gaze as he continued, "But first, you had to be brought together with that objective in mind, and I chose to effectuate the session in a way that would cause the least harm to you."

"Lying to me was the least harm? You said you'd help keep me awake during the last session. Did you lie about that too?"

"No. Other than the suicide—which I remind you, did indeed happen—I have been completely up-front and honest with you, Mr. Crawford."

"Really?"

"Yes. And as for conditioning you to remain conscious during your hypnotic session with Dr. Romero, I did that to protect you; it made sure you were not deceived any more. Did you lose consciousness or fail to recall what occurred while the session was in progress?"

"That's the thing: I don't know. I saw the flashing thingamajig on his desk, and—"

"Are you referring to the hypno-strobe? If so, the mere fact that you remember it at all demonstrates that you must have been fully conscious. Every therapist knows to cloak the existence of the hypno-strobe from the patient; that is standard procedure. So, you see, that is proof that I did not lie to you about that."

"Maybe not, but when were you planning on telling me that Dr. Romero was really my own aunt?" I wasn't sure if the word I intended to say as "aunt" came out sounding like "mother," but for the purposes of my conversation with Dr. Simmons, it ultimately didn't matter.

"Oh, my. Did she tell you?"

"No, she didn't, and neither did you."

"Please, Mr. Crawford: Try to understand. She was my colleague here at the clinic. Such a revelation could cause irreparable damage to you and your psychological well-being."

"You don't have to tell me, Doc. The damage has been done."

"I can't begin to fathom, without her telling you, how you managed to figure it out, to pierce the veil of her manufactured persona. As a therapist who relies on hypnotism myself, I would have thought it impossible."

"And I ain't done piercing veils just yet. I will tell you that I figured it out by recording that session. When I played it back, it wasn't Dr. Romero's voice. Care to guess whose voice it was?"

"Your mother's voice?"

"No, even though my brother insists that it was. No, Dr. Simmons, it turned out, at least to my ear, that it was your voice. How do you account for that?" I stared into the eyes across the desk and, failing to recognize even a glimmer of familiarity, I demanded, "Is that you, Auntie?"

"Mr. Crawford! I realize this matter has proven most bewildering for you, but do make an effort to approach this with some semblance of reason rather than emotion."

"You didn't answer my question."

"I am not your mother, Mr. Crawford. I have no ready explanation for why you heard my voice in place of someone else's. Although, if I ponder it a bit further, I may yet have an answer that, come to think of it, makes perfect sense."

"Well, while you're thinking up another lie, maybe you can explain why your office voicemail greeting is still the same as that actor you hired, yet the reporter I had working on this case insists it's your voice. Huh?"

"That is what I was about to clarify for you, Mr. Crawford. What goes on in a therapy session is sacrosanct. It is privileged and must remain private. Do you realize that every patient who walks into a therapist's office has a smartphone and is thus armed with the latest recording technology? I am sure that is what you used to record your sessions, was it not? To safeguard against abuse, it has become standard operating procedure industry-wide to utilize what is called a 'MARV' or misdirected alternative recorded voice. If a patient happens to record a session surreptitiously, they will not hear the therapist's voice but an alternative that the therapist has earlier implanted."

"Another mind manipulation?"

"Yes, in a sense. But it is to protect both the patient as well as the doctor. In this case, I did change my office voicemail greeting. It was a coincidence that I had established a MARV using the voice of the actor that you told me you had already heard. I assure you, it is my voice now."

"I'd ask you to prove it, but I first want to know how you can explain that I hear your voice—the one I'm hearing now—on that recording of Dr. Romero, which is to say, my aunt. Explain that one."

"It is not at all unusual for a therapist to establish a MARV that points to the patient's previous or last-known therapist. Your mother would simply instruct you, under hypnosis, that if you ever heard her recorded voice played back, you would hear the voice of the last therapist with whom you had spoken or been treated. Ironically, that happened to be me."

"I'll have to think about that. You're just full of good answers, aren't you? Then answer this: When Amy, my reporter, came to see you, she told me you said you had never heard of me—why would you say that?"

"I am not in the habit of discussing my patients with others, least of all, inquisitive reporters. I realized immediately that you had gone against my wishes in contacting the press, and I chose not to divulge our relationship. I trust you have at least some modicum of respect for my discretion."

"Okay, let's say I believe you. Tell me one more thing: If I came back to this same office tomorrow, would I see you sitting in that chair or would I see someone else?"

"My dear Mr. Crawford, surely you must already know the answer to that question. Because our relationship is clandestine, I would have no choice but to disavow it publicly. And as for my appearance, although I assure you that I am who I say, you are well acquainted with the power of mental conditioning. You harbor some suspicion that I am not as I appear to you now. How easy would it be to have you see and hear the very same guise in whoever you may meet in this chair tomorrow? In either case, you will see what you expect to see. And as personal descriptions are inescapably subjective, you would not be able to expose any discrepancies by comparing your own perceptions—as locked-in as they are—with those of others. A lifelong career in psychology has taught me that such is the nature of the mind."

"And what about my memories?" I asked, my voice quivering with desperation.

"That our memories are truly our own is utterly a myth. It is, indeed, the conceit of memory. Our experiences are subject to both interpretations and influences whose sources are hidden in the murky background of our environment, both physical and social. My role as a therapist is helping my patients to embrace the 'fluidity' of their existence, and having accepted it, to go on to lead meaningful and fulfilling lives."

I inwardly bristled at the notion that anyone could find "meaning" in a life that had been as manipulated and contorted as my own. Despite my initial resistance, I allowed myself to absorb the words that Dr. Simmons had just shared with me. As I reflected further, those words seemed fraught with wisdom. I sensed that soldiering on through the narrow tunnel of acceptance would prove for me to be the only way out of the mess I was in and the only way forward.

After I expressed my begrudging gratitude, we shook hands with indifference, and I walked out of the office. As I left the building, I knew in my gut that I would never return to the clinic or any other like it. The psychiatric system had become tainted for me. I acknowledged that people like Dr. Simmons might be genuine in trying to help people with their problems, and I took no issue with that. But the methods these practitioners used were not far removed from the barbarism of the Inquisition, even if they were mental rather than physical devices. And as an undeniable victim of the frank abuse of those methods, I had come to reject the system altogether. Leaving the clinic that day, I had never felt so alone in this brutal, miserable world of ours.

20

Learning about Auntie

The feeling of isolation I first felt after leaving the clinic carried over to the following day. I awoke like a man who had slept for a hundred years, struggling to come to life and perplexed by his surroundings. Stirring through the mist of my mental fog, I found myself in the familiar confines of my apartment, but it was a starkly different atmosphere, for its rooms had come to be haunted by the presence of a man who had seemingly lost his soul.

I checked my smartphone for messages and saw that Matt had texted me at one o'clock in the morning, asking how things had gone. It amused me to think what kind of text message I could send in reply that would convey what I had learned from Dr. Simmons, about both myself and our aunt. I reflected on whether to call Matt but decided this wasn't a topic for phone conversation either. I pecked out a simple text reply, "Come on over." I didn't wait for a response. I laid the device down, took a hot shower, and ate a little breakfast.

I checked my smartphone again. Matt still hadn't texted. I took the opportunity to call in sick for the day at work. Fortunately, I reached my boss' voicemail and left a message. If I were later asked what my ailment had been, I was more than prepared to answer "blown mind." I never did quite understand how anyone could expect horses to piece together eggshells: Hooves aren't as useful for grasping as hands with opposable thumbs. Of course, the King's men fared no better.

How I had changed when it came to my work ethic. Where once I had been so reliable at work that I had received the most "Employee of the Month" awards of anyone in the region, I had become reliable only in the very spottiness of my attendance. So much had happened to me in such a brief time: losing Bianca in the worst way; re-entering the clutches of Dr. Romero, whoever he turned out to be; getting hornswoggled by Dr. Simmons; and discovering my whole life had been one enormous lie. The recent ordeal of it all had stripped me of my personal motivation to succeed, at work and in life.

The distinct rhythm of the knock at the door interrupted my thoughts and signaled that Matt had arrived. I didn't bother to look through the peephole but just opened the door widely. There in the doorway stood my new-found brother, as if in a picture frame, hand on hip, staring blankly forward, like a modern-day Blue Boy, all the more reminiscent of the painting, clad in a dark-blue shirt and blue jeans.

"Yo, 'sup," said Matt in his endearing fashion, as he waltzed into my apartment. I closed the door behind him without returning a greeting because I wanted to show him how serious I was; this was no social call to hang out: My life was at stake, and once again, I looked to him for help.

I gestured for him to take a seat on the sofa, while I grimly sat in an adjacent chair. My mind fumbled for the right words to express the news I was desperate to share with Matt, or at that point, with anyone, really.

Matt spoke with exasperation in his voice, "Dude, it's me: your brother. Just tell me, nice and slow, what went down with your other shrink last night. Okay?"

I told him the whole story, from my talk with Amy, right through to my final encounter with Dr. Simmons. Reviewing it aloud and hearing the details in my own voice renewed my astonishment at what I had been subjected to, not merely over the last several weeks, but for my whole life. The emotions I felt as I recounted the story spanned the gamut, from self-pity to a frightening thirst for revenge. When I was done speaking, I was exhausted and emotionally drained. I found Matt's response, wide-eyed with mouth slightly agape in apparent disbelief, to be nothing less than appropriate.

"The one thing I regret," I said, "was not asking Dr. Simmons' advice on whether I ought to confront Auntie about all this."

"I'm still not sure if Simmons is legit. If Auntie could catfish you as Romero, why not as Simmons?"

"Yeah, but don't you see: It doesn't really matter. Let's say Auntie were, in fact, the real person behind the Simmons mask; then, asking Simmons is the same as asking Auntie. And if not, I'd still have gotten some good advice."

"Hey, it looks like I'm the only one you have left to turn to for advice. How sad is that?" Matt frowned and then continued, "But, in my opinion, I think it was good you didn't ask Simmons about having it out with Auntie. If it really was her, you would have lost the element of surprise. And this is something you're going to want to spring on her, don't you think?"

"I honestly haven't decided yet whether I'm going to say a word to her. If I got anything from that last meeting with Simmons, it was more about accepting things the way they are than seeking some pointless revenge."

"Who said anything about revenge? I'm just saying, if it were me, I'd hash it out with her. Plus, don't you need her to, like, release you or something?"

"You are so right, Matt. That's exactly what I need to do. I'll worry later about whether I can forgive her for what she did, but I need to give her an opportunity to set things right. Thanks—again—for talking sense to me."

"That's what a smarter little brother is for, man." Matt smirked before asking, "Do you want me to be there when you face her, because I can, or do you want to go it alone?"

"I appreciate your offer, but I need to do this on my own."

We hugged, and as he was leaving, Matt impressed on me that I was to let him know how it went. I owed him that much, since I was the one who had brought him into my mess, starting with asking him to be my best man at the wedding and on through helping me record my session with the erstwhile Dr. Romero. Without his help and support throughout my ordeal, I wouldn't have made any progress, not to mention the discoveries and insights that had helped me unravel the mystery of what had happened to me. At that moment, as I closed the door behind him, I felt I still had a chance, however slim, at a happy future.

I sank back into the sofa to think things over, but I knew deep down that what I was doing served no purpose other than postponing my inevitable encounter with Auntie. *I had been her pawn since the age of five, I thought, so why not wait another day or two, or even a week?* Any doctor would say that I had been through a lot emotionally in the last couple of days, so taking a break to allow those wounds to heal would not be all that unreasonable.

It's amazing how people tended to rationalize any decision, any action, or in my case, any lack of action. *No, I promised myself, I would not live another day under the oppressive psychological prescription of a madwoman, aunt or no aunt.* I grabbed my phone and called Auntie immediately, without giving any prior thought to what I was going to say or how I was going to come across.

It rang only once. The caller ID with my name must have displayed on her end, since she answered, her voice dripping with honey, as soon as the call connected, "Trevor, darling, it always warms my heart to hear from you. What is my son up to these days?"

As I held the phone to my ear, I resisted with all my might to respond by telling her I wasn't her son. *Had she programmed me to resist that?* I wondered, *and would the word "son" even come out of my mouth as I intended?* I calmed myself and said, "We need to talk. Are you going to be at home for a while?"

"Yes, I am at home, but I have plans to go out this afternoon."

"Do not move. I will be right over." I didn't wait for a response before ending the call. Upon further reflection, I wished I hadn't been so gruff and un-loving; it would tip her off that I was onto her charade and was coming to confront her. I hadn't heeded Matt's advice about the element of surprise. This could only provide her time to think up some explanation or to leave and not be there when I arrived. *What if I went to her house and found only a note?* It was too late. The best I could do was get over to her house quickly before she had time to think or act. Suppressing any further thoughts, I was out the door in no time.

My apartment was situated closer to the city center, albeit far from downtown, but it was only a short drive to the residential side of town where Auntie lived. Entering the suburbs, with its quiet, tree-lined streets and slow-paced pedestrians, was like entering another world. Thanks to the mid-morning hour of the day, I was able to park my car right in front of Auntie's house. Her own car was parked in her driveway, so I was fairly certain she was still at home.

As I strode up the walkway, I saw the front door inch open, and Auntie stood in the doorway to welcome me. She was smiling, perhaps even beaming, full of pride, the way I imagine only a mother could fully express. *Is this how a fly is drawn in*, I wondered, *when it stumbles into a spider's web*? I momentarily regretted that I hadn't taken the time to mentally prepare myself, to fortify my mind, so to speak, before venturing into the lion's lair. My muscles tensed in every quadrant of my body, from legs to arms to clenched teeth, as I girded myself for the looming encounter. *I will not lose my temper*, I told myself, *nor be less than kind.*

"Dearest Trevor, you sounded so stressed over the phone," she said, holding her arms out for an anticipated hug. She first looked me up and down, saying, "You're looking fine, my boy." When we embraced, she asked, "What's wrong?"

I stood in the entryway as she closed the door but then proceeded to move to the adjacent living room and took a seat. She sat on the sofa, on the end next to my chair. The angle this created between us did not comfortably accommodate our looking each other face-to-face, but I wasn't sure at that point I even wanted to view her any other way than out of the corner of my eye. As awkward as it was, we did somehow manage to maintain eye contact. She placed her hand on my knee and repeated her question, "What's wrong?"

"Auntie, I know. I know all about Dr. Romero."

"I'm so sorry, Trevor. I could kick myself for recommending that your Uncle Joe take you to see that quack.

He wasn't even trained to treat children, especially my sweet little boy."

She reached out, as if to touch my face. I recoiled and moved my head backward to avoid any contact. "Stop it! Stop it. Quit pretending, for crying out loud. I know it was you. I don't quite know how you did it, but you made me believe you were him. And in the process, you ruined my life."

"Oh, my dear boy, I don't know what you think you know, but whatever I did, I did it to protect you. I wish you could see that."

"Then explain it to me. Matt and I figured some of it out. You had no children of your own, so you had to 'steal' one from your own brother."

She crossed her arms and threw her head back haughtily. "Did you get little Matt involved in this? Now I'll have to work on him next."

"You stay away from him! Haven't you done enough damage?"

"It's quite the contrary. I feel like I've been on 'damage control' for the last twenty years. Do you have any idea how hard it's been to engineer this masquerade and keep it a secret? I'm a lot smarter than you think, dear boy."

In my anguish, I had to chuckle at the thought that she seemed somehow to be fishing for a compliment. *Was I supposed to admire how "smart" she had been in manipulating my memory and identity?* There might be a thin line between genius and madness, but no one had told me until I discovered it myself how delicate the boundary could be between brilliance and malevolence. The same was also true of tragedy and comedy, the theatrical twins who, like mythological muses, take turns bedeviling human lives. At that moment, the whole situation was so epic, yet at its core, so pitiful, that I couldn't help but see it with a perverse sort of bemusement. I continued to chuckle.

Auntie picked up on my snicker and began to imitate it. Perhaps she thought that, if we could find a way to laugh at it, maybe I wouldn't think that what she'd done was so bad after all. Her chuckle progressed into a cackle, which made her appear even more evil than I would've dared imagine.

I turned serious. "Look, I'm here to ask—no, demand—that you make amends. You can start by 'fessing up, and not just to me but to the whole family. I still can't believe Mom and Dad didn't know. That word-substitution thing, where I'd say one word but hear another… That was indeed clever. But it's time everyone knows what you did to me."

"You must think I'm the most selfish person in the world. Well, for once, I'm going to put this family's welfare ahead of my own. That means I will most definitely not be destroying everyone you and I both love by telling them our secret. And for what? Because you think you'll feel better afterward. Trust me, you won't."

I resisted her attempt to turn things around and somehow make me the bad guy. "Trust you? I don't even trust my own memories, let alone the manipulative witch who planted them in my head."

"That's what I'm saying, Trevor. I know you're angry. You have every right to be. I'm not asking for forgiveness. What I'm saying is, don't act out of anger. Don't let it darken your heart to the point where you'd sacrifice your family just to avenge the wrong I did you."

Hearing her finally declare that she'd wronged me seemed to soften my resolve. It forced me to consider, *How would putting the whole family through the proverbial wringer undo the pain that I alone had suffered?* I was shocked to come to the realization that she was probably right and that whatever amends she made would have to be in holes and corners.

With a sense of resignation, I sighed and then asked, "What about Matt?" I didn't wait for a response before adding, "He knows. He helped me figure it out."

"I'll fix it. The less you know about it, the better."

"I cannot stomach the idea of your manipulating his memories like you did mine. Maybe I can convince him to keep quiet; that way, you won't have to trick him."

"No. He would slip up sometime, and I don't mean he'd do so intentionally. On top of that, should we expect him to carry the weight of this secret forever? Don't you want him to be unburdened? He deserves that, Trevor. You know I'm correct about that."

"I suppose so," I said, the words accompanied by another less-than-voluntary sigh. I didn't feel that my encounter with Auntie was progressing as I had expected. So far, I had managed, first of all, to extract a private admission of guilt, although how precisely she had wronged me had been left unsaid. Second, I had allowed her to plan on letting Matt off the hook using her mind-control techniques, something to which I previously could never have imagined agreeing. *Was that it? I wondered. Was that as far as I was going to go in demanding that she make amends?*

A blood-chilling thought occurred to me as I reflected on others whose lives she had touched. "What about Emily?" I asked. "Do you realize what you did to her? I mean, to her through me?"

"Now, you hold on there," she said, wagging her right index finger. "I blocked that memory for years, just to spare you the heartache."

"Yeah, the heartache of thinking how close I came to being intimate with my own—"

She allowed me to trail off, but then, as if belatedly to help me complete my sentence, she said, "Cousin?"

"You're not my mother, so what are you saying?"

"What if Emily were actually my daughter? That would make you cousins, just like you thought. No?"

"That's a lie. Why, Auntie? Why can't you stop lying to me?"

"I didn't lie. I was just asking a question. But don't you see? I can't help myself whenever I see you're hurting. I just want to protect you, Trevor, from all the pain around you."

"If that's true, then why did Dr. Romero—I mean, you—force me to remember that terrible memory I'd forgotten? You did that. Why?"

"I only allowed you to remember it so you'd get back together with your fiancée."

"Oh, yeah: my fiancée. Did you force me into thinking I loved Bianca, or was that for real? I hear you saying you want us back together, but then why, for the love of Pete, did you embarrass me at my own wedding? That's something I just don't understand."

"You have to believe me when I tell you that it wasn't what I had planned. I embedded the conditioning trigger when you were a boy. I thought, 'I can't lose my son to the first woman he meets.' And I know you, Trevor. You were always so easy to impress. I didn't plan for it to happen with Bianca."

"You were sitting right there in the church and watched it happen. What do you mean you didn't plan for it? You saw your plan unfold right before your eyes. Do you have any idea what that did to me? Do you even care?"

"I love you, Trevor. Of course, I care. And it's true: I planted the idea in your mind to fall in love with Bianca, but you were just infatuated. You don't know what real love is."

"And you do?"

"I know what it is to love someone, because I have loved you for your entire life." She took a deep breath and smiled, an expression that had come to look maniacal to me, as she continued, "I could say you were the son I never had, but the reality is that I did have you, after all."

I could feel the tears welling up in my eyes. As one tear fell, I could feel the coolness of it as it descended my warm cheek. I was determined not to break down and cry, since it would only signal weakness, as though she still wielded control over me. I had to shake them off, both her influence and the tears it had engendered.

I spoke again, my voice cracking ever so slightly, saying, "If you're ready to make amends, you can start by patching things up between me and Bianca. I think if you confess everything to her, she will—"

"Oh, no, we're over Bianca. When I saw how that father of hers treated you, I knew it had to end. He would have made your life miserable. When I first met Bianca, I thought, 'What a lovely girl for my Trevor. Maybe I should remove the trigger?' But not if it would make you miserable. No, sir."

"Who the blazes do you think you are? Is everyone just a pawn in your little game? You decide who I should marry and then you decide I shouldn't. If you can't see how terrible that is, then I'm not sure how I'm ever going to forgive you, Auntie… not in this lifetime, anyway."

"Oh, Trevor, I'm your—" It was obvious that force of habit was about to make her say the word "mother," but she caught herself, probably realizing how it would make me feel at that moment. She resumed, "Let me tell you about a man I met a long time ago named Ted Crawford."

"There really is a man named Crawford?"

"Yes." She looked off into space, as if trying to recall a distant memory.

We had been making eye contact constantly up to that point, and as she averted her gaze, my muscles relaxed and I found myself open to listening to her story. "Go on," I said.

"You have to realize that, twenty-five years ago, all I had was my career."

She went on to explain that Ted Crawford was enlisted in the Army and came to her as a patient, suffering from post-traumatic stress disorder, or PTSD. During the war, the Army recruited the services of local psychologists to treat those afflicted with the disorder prior to their redeployment for additional tours of duty. The treatments, whether effective or not, were therefore under a deadline.

I had a hard time imagining Auntie in the flowering of her youth, but she told me how she had come to fall in love with Ted, despite the ethical implications of violating a doctor-patient trust with a personal affair. As I listened, I couldn't help but wonder what Dr. Simmons, who had seemed to fancy himself the standard-bearer for professional ethics and the prosecutor of physician misconduct, would have said about such an affair.

She had never been in love before, or for that matter, since. I could not help but be struck by how passionately she described having met the love of her life and their plans to marry upon his return from his next tour.

After he was shipped off to the combat zone, they communicated often, either through letters or phone calls he was allowed to make off-base during periodic leaves.

"I felt a connection with him," she said, "that I had never experienced before. It was as though I felt his presence, even when we were apart."

Several weeks into their separation, Auntie found out she was pregnant. She considered telling Ted but decided not to give him anything more to worry about on the battlefield; in fact, she was concerned that, if she told him, he would desert in order to be by her side. "That's the kind of guy he was," she said.

Because they weren't yet married and weren't otherwise related, the Army had no reason to notify her of Ted's status. She read in the newspaper that he had been killed in action, presumably under hostile fire.

She was so devastated by the news that her knees buckled and she took a tumble down a flight of stairs. Although she emerged from the fall relatively unscathed, she miscarried and lost their unborn child. The Ax of Fate had proved to be double-edged: the same day she learned that it had robbed her of her soul mate, it took the mortal being of the life they had created together and by which she could have hoped to remember him. She also learned she would never be able to conceive again.

While describing the events, Auntie had clutched one of the throw pillows on the couch and was embracing it as she rocked on the edge of the sofa. Her eyes squinted, as if she were squeezing out the tears that were by then, and without any overt sign of effort on her part, rolling down her cheeks. It was the first time in a long time I had seen her show any real emotion.

I mused over the notion that the only way to soften one's thirst for revenge might be to conjure feelings of empathy for those who have wronged you. I found myself, quite contrary to my expectation, on the emotional on-ramp of that narrowest of high-ways, the road to forgiveness.

She told me how she had begun experimenting with self-hypnosis, at first trying to induce an amnesia that would rid her of the painful memories she was experiencing. Whether those efforts failed or whether she abandoned them didn't matter; she decided that she preferred an eventful, albeit agonizing, life to a stoic one.

In the aftermath of her grief, her brother and his wife—my mom and dad—consoled her. She came to our house numerous times during that period, and on one such occasion, she remembered seeing me at play. Something about the color of my eyes and hair, which were different from those of my siblings, bore a striking resemblance for her to Ted's. In the maelstrom of her emotions, having lost her lover and baby, along with her own experiments in hypnosis and memory manip-ulation, a desperate thought had occurred to her to find a way to claim me in place of her missing child. She ra-tionalized that she was merely grafting a twig from the same family tree.

"My womb would never be ready for motherhood, but at that moment, my heart ached for it," she said.

Her emotional need inspired her to envision an elaborate scheme involving identity masking and word switching that she could use to ensnare me into her fab-ricated world, the one in which she became the mother that fate had robbed her of being. Rather than feeling the anger that had driven me to confront Auntie in the first place, I felt instead a gnawing sense of pity: a coldly comforting compassion.

"I can't be something I never was," I told her.

"Yes, I understand that now. I so regret that, in laboring to ease my own suffering, I've ended up hurting others, especially my own family. I never meant to hurt you, Trevor. You must accept that. It's the truth."

Even though I had mistrusted her, I witnessed genuineness in Auntie's tears and in her belated remorse. I refocused our attention on what had brought me to her house that day. I said, "But part of making amends, Auntie, is that you've got to undo all this stuff you planted in my mind. You're the only one who can do that. If you release me, I can get on with my life; and if that works out, I will try with all my might someday to forgive you. But you have to undo it, Auntie, you simply have to."

"You're asking me to give up my child again. I know you aren't biologically my son, but the love I felt for you: That was always real." She clasped her right hand closed and rapped her chest with it repeatedly. "I got a chance to feel what a mother feels. There is no greater love in this world than a mother's love."

"Don't you care at all about my happiness?"

"Oh, Trevor, that's all I ever wanted. For the sake of your happiness, and only for that, I would be willing to give up being a mother. Isn't it ironic, though?"

"What?"

"To avoid the feeling of having lost a child, I now have to endure the loss twice. But you know, I think I'm finally ready to grieve. I'm ready to let go."

I knew from my own experience that pent-up feelings were apt to erupt and that, as a consequence, a reaction could appear out-of-proportion to the circumstances. Almost instinctively, I grabbed her shoulders to draw her into an embrace. She hugged me back, gripping me tightly, with more strength than I would have expected for such an otherwise diminutive woman.

She said, "I promise I'll make it right, and we can be a family again, a real family." Our hug ended, we reclined back into our respective seats.

"Are you coming to the barbecue tomorrow?" I asked, referring to the annual family get-together for the upcoming holiday. Dad always felt that we were all so scattered, living our own lives, that once a year, he would insist on having under one roof all the people he loved and cared about. This included Mom, of course, in addition to us kids, Dad's sister, their elderly aunt, and a couple of distant cousins. It was the one time we all celebrated being a family, so it was all the more important that I be there as myself, his eldest son, not as his nephew foster son.

"Of course, I'm coming. The last time we were all together was for that horrible wedding of yours. Praise be that we weren't joined with that family!" She must have seen the renewed anger in my face, because she changed topics without missing a beat. "It will be nice sharing the holiday together as a family."

She grabbed my wrist and reeled me in for another hug. I let the embrace go on for a while but finally interrupted it by saying, "Auntie? It's time for you to let me go."

She wiped away her tears and sat up straight as if to gather herself. She spoke slowly, in measured tones, and with deliberateness and clarity. "I have a fail-safe phrase to disengage all of the protocols. I had planned to say it on my deathbed. I was always worried that you'd have trouble adjusting afterward. But I can tell, you'll be just fine, because like me, you're a survivor."

"Am I going to forget everything that's happened? Is that how it works?"

"In a way, but your memory will actually be redirected. We never truly forget: We can only control the manner by which we recall our memories. The final protocol—the fail-safe—will block your remembering any of it in either thought or speech. When you physically write it down, with pen and paper, however, then, and only then, will you remember it."

"So, if I ever write a book about this, I'll be able to remember all of it, but otherwise, you're saying that I won't?"

"Yes. And the same for Matt. It's your only way forward."

She lifted a large bound book with a title embossed in gold on its cover from the coffee table by where we were sitting and handed it to me. It had been sitting there all along without my noticing it. I riffled through it and saw that all the pages were blank, in the manner of a diary. I didn't think much of it but held it close to me, nonetheless.

"So, once you say the fail-safe phrase, I can get my life back?"

"Uh huh. Now, do be aware that you might be confused at first, but once you work through stitching the various memory fragments together, you'll eventually stabilize. About the fail-safe phrase… I had to pick something unique that you weren't apt to encounter on your own in your everyday life."

"Okay, what is it?"

"My original choice for something you'd probably never hear in your lifetime was 'The Chicago Cubs just won the World Series,' but then I wondered what would happen if those suckers actually pulled it off someday."

"Auntie, I don't need a history lesson or the story behind how you chose the words I need to hear." *The suspense was killing me.* "Just say it. Tell me the fail-safe phrase now, please."

I saw her mouthing something, although I couldn't be sure if that was how it happened or simply the way I'd later recall the moment. Perhaps my not remembering having heard the words was part of the intended effect of hearing them. So went all the experiences of humanity: The mind tended to invent wherever it lacked understanding. In any case, what she mouthed impressed me as a nonsensical incantation, akin to a German poem about a cuckoo I'd heard as a young boy that went something like: *Sim salabim bam bah sala du saladim.* I was awed by both the mystery and power of such words, as well as of the liberating effect they could have on an oppressed mind.

21

Becoming a family

I could offer no accounting for what happened after Auntie spoke her fail-safe phrase to me. In fact, until I sat, with pen in hand, to write about my experiences, I had no recollection of any of the events I'd recorded in the diary-like volume she gave me. Having lived a mostly digital life, I had grown unaccustomed to writing long paragraphs by hand. Sure, there was paperwork at the bank, but most of the documents were digitized, and my job did consist of occasional hand-written addenda. Unfortunately, the mental recall didn't work if I typed or used a recording device, so I had no choice but to write everything by hand with an ink pen. The cramps in my hand would attest to my efforts.

If anyone might be reading these words, I'd reckon it likely that my journal found its way to publication. Perhaps lessons could be learned from its pages and the experiences chronicled therein.

The following morning, I awakened without the benefit of an alarm clock, which I had remembered to switch off on account of the holiday. I was actually looking forward to the annual barbecue that our family had turned into something of our own holiday. I had always been a member of the family, but this time, I would take the stage as the eldest son, and my brother and sister would be right there beside me. I relished the prospect of a new, first-time experience in the midst of a life over which I'd grown weary. I wasn't yet thirty years old, but it had been a tumultuous albeit brief, and otherwise mundane, life up to that point. I delighted in the prospect of a better one to come.

I kept the bound journal on my nightstand so that it was within easy reach on those many nights I had trouble sleeping. When I picked it up, I felt its leather-like covering; the taut softness of the texture was soothing to the touch. I would read its ironic, gold-lettered title: Dream Journal. *Was that Auntie's twisted sense of humor?* If only it had all been a dream, it would not be still haunting me. I reflected on how all the important pieces of my life—family, work, and even my love life—had all been carefully orchestrated in accordance with her fiendish, decades-long, psychology experiment.

What if Auntie had lied and I were still operating under some kind of post-hypnotic suggestion? I wondered. *What was real and what wasn't? Could a man, with only his own strength and mental fortitude, overcome the grip of conditioning and succeed in asserting his own individuality?*

I decided to allow myself the opportunity to live my life, oblivious to the hurtful and manipulative experiences that had once controlled it. *Unless we're prepared to confront the memory of those experiences and make them part of ourselves*, I reasoned, *perhaps it would be wise not to question where they came from.* The one indisputable conclusion that I could draw from my ordeal was that, simply stated, *you are who you are*, and there could be no useful purpose in trying to unravel all the "whys" and the "what ifs."

I shook the sleepy cobwebs from my head. One of the first things that occurred to me to do that morning was to call Bianca and invite her to come with me to the barbecue. In my non-writing state of amnesia, my recollections of events had evolved to a point of consistency. That had been the key—consistency—for only with that could the brain grapple with its representation of reality. I had an inkling that our wedding had been a disaster but couldn't recall the exact reason. Despite the vast number of onlookers to witness what had actually happened, etiquette and decorum prevented any of them from coming forward or sharing with me their perspectives. In such a fog and isolation, my psyche had been given a chance to heal itself.

I didn't feel bitter about not marrying Bianca, because whenever I searched in my heart—whether with the awareness of writing or in the obliviousness of thought—I knew we no longer loved each other, if indeed we ever did. It was like losing a piece of costume jewelry: The sense of loss might be undeniable, but the impact of the loss would not be lasting or truly mourned.

When I reached Bianca by phone, I jabbered some tepid apology, even though, as I voiced it, I did not fully appreciate why I was sorry. She thanked me for the good times we had had together and for the sense of adventure our courtship had brought into her life. She went on to explain that her father had already arranged a suitable replacement for me in the form of a dashing young man from a wealthy and privileged family not unlike her own. She had taken a liking to him, she said, and could envision a wedding with him in the not-too-distant future. I was happy for her. The thought then of inviting her to the barbecue seemed altogether inappropriate. We said our goodbyes for what I knew in my heart would likely be the final time. I was glad to hear that she had landed on her feet and had moved on so quickly from our engagement.

It dawned on me that I could bring Amy to the barbecue instead. I knew she would hate being an afterthought; the mental image of her glaring at me for having landed on my plate as a backup or second choice almost dissuaded me from giving her a call. But I dialed her number anyway, and when she answered, and I got to hear her voice again, I felt a kind of warmth inside, what I'd describe as a "coziness" or comfortable familiarity. I did not have to hesitate around her or sugarcoat my intentions: She made it apparent that she liked the direct approach, and she gave as "good" as she got.

It was such short notice that I didn't allow myself to be disappointed when, as expected, she declined my invitation. Nor did that frame of mind dampen my elation when she suggested we have lunch the following week to make up for the lunch date we'd missed. I accepted without much fanfare. Had I permitted my emotions to bubble to the surface, I would have screamed "Yes," but I was savvy enough to know that such a response would have reeked of desperation. To be "cool," one must exude indifference, even as one's heart is about to leap with eagerness from one's chest.

As we said our goodbyes and ended our call, I realized that, for the first time in a long while, I had something to look forward to. The door had closed on my relationship with Bianca, but a window had opened—ever so slightly—of some kind of future with Amy.

As my thoughts turned toward going stag to the barbecue, my mood turned solemn, but I felt strangely unburdened. I yearned to share that feeling with everyone I met. I hadn't seen Mom and Dad or Emily since Auntie's revelation, and I was anxious to head over to the barbecue in my new role as devoted son and brother. Of course, I had to keep in mind that the role was new only to me; the others had always seen me for what I truly was.

I drove across town to the same residential area where Auntie resided, and as I maneuvered the car to park in front of the familiar house where Mom and Dad lived, I saw shadowy figures briskly moving about busily inside. Where once I would have politely knocked at the door as the foster child, I seized the doorknob and walked right in.

Through the glass door at the rear of the house, visible from the entryway where I stood, I could see into the back yard, darkened by the mid-day shadow of an enormous banner, hung above the fence, that read: WILKINS Family Bar-B-Q. I didn't need to remind myself that I was indeed, and always had been, a Wilkins.

On the rare occasions that I encountered the name "Crawford," as it might rarely come across my desk at work in a loan application, unless I were actively writing, it evoked no reaction in me nor sense of familiarity. Although I had come to forgive Auntie for what she had done—and I was blessed to not recall her actions except when writing—I marveled at the scope of the damage she caused, to me personally, to all my relationships, and to our family.

Out of the corner of my eye, to the right of the entryway, I caught a glimpse of the back wall of the hallway, as always adorned with framed pictures of the many family outings throughout the years I grew up in the house. To my amazement, I couldn't find one in which Auntie appeared, a fact that I hadn't previously noticed. One picture in particular drew my attention—it was of Mom and Dad, along with us three kids, during an early summer camping trip. I must have walked past that picture thousands of times on the way to school, but it was as if I was looking at it anew. Before, I had felt like a visitor, albeit a rather permanent one, in the Wilkins' household. The theme was familiar: Here was Uncle Joe, his wife, their two children, and the foster child they had taken in. At that moment, as I studied the picture, I realized for the first time in my life that I was at the center of it, both literally and figuratively: a close-knit family, proudly surrounding the oldest son, who should never have felt like he was an outsider.

I began walking from the hallway into the family room to reach the back yard beyond, when my mom emerged from the kitchen, carrying party supplies and plates of food in her arms, and greeted me, "Trevor! You're here early."

I took some of the items she was carrying to relieve her load and was about to speak with her, but she scurried out to the backyard to set down the remaining items on the picnic table there. I followed her and helped set the table for the day's upcoming festivities. Toward the back right of the yard I saw the free-standing grill, puffs of white, papal-like smoke already ascending from it. The smell of grilled food filled my nostrils and seemed to permeate the entire area; a tangy scent cut the sweet odor of molasses, and the combination made my mouth water. In front of the grill was Dad, wearing a white chef's hat, a white apron knotted in the back, and, incongruously, a pair of khaki shorts.

"Mom, I know you're busy, but I have something important to tell you."

She set down the utensils she was placing and looked into my face. "Is it about Bianca?" she asked, with some excitement in her voice. "Were you two able to patch things up? If you love her, don't give up, Trevor. Just don't."

"No, No," I shook my head, "it's over. And you know what? I'm glad it is. Quite frankly, I'm relieved about it. We were never meant to be together."

"But, sweetheart, you were about to marry her. You were so sure that she was the one. Of course, if you don't love her anymore, well, then—"

"I realized that I never did. There was something from my past that made me think I was in love with her, or in fact, what she represents. But I sorted it out, and I decided—we both decided—we were from different worlds."

"I want you to be happy," she said. "And I know for certain you'll find the right one. Don't let this discourage you. It's not always love-at-first-sight, you know."

"Was it for you and Dad?"

She looked across the yard at Dad, in his shorts, sweating in front of the grill. "Yes, I suppose it was." She smiled broadly. "At least, for me. I pretty much had to convince your father that he too loved me from the moment we met, but I bet he did anyway."

"Let's ask him… Hey, Dad!" I shouted. "Did you love Mom from the moment you laid eyes on her?"

He was some distance away and turned his head, not quite in our direction but, as if to prick up his ears. He shouted back, "Laid 'what' on her?" He didn't wait for an answer and turned back to attend to the grill.

Mom and I shrugged our shoulders, nearly simultaneously, before I said to her, "Well, it doesn't matter how it happens. Next time, though, I'm going to pick a girl who's just like you, because I love you,

Mom." I didn't know whether my own words served as a cue or if I simply felt it had been a long time, but I opened my arms and pulled her in close to me for a hug. After all I had been through recently, I felt more emotional, more passionate. I squeezed her in something of a bear hug, perhaps a little too tightly, although I would wager very few mothers would call any loving embrace of their children uncomfortable or in any way unwelcome.

Mom hugged me back and seemed unable to hold back a dainty little laugh, probably at the strength of the wrestler-style hug in which I had her. She said, "Sweet child, you always were so sensitive and thoughtful." She touched the back of my head, in a tender way that only she could. I released her, or rather, we released each other, and she took a step backward into a more relaxed stance. She remarked, "Speaking of resemblance, I've begun to notice that I sure do see a lot of myself in Emily. I was just like her at that age."

"Where is Emily?"

"She called earlier to say Matt was picking her up, which means they probably won't be here for a while—"

Just as Mom was speaking, Matt and Emily emerged from the sliding-glass door to make their way into the backyard toward us at the table. I was certain Matt's speedy car, not to mention his lead foot, accounted for their unexpectedly early arrival. We greeted and hugged one another; when Matt first offered his hand, seemingly to initiate a handshake with me, I used his arm instead to pull him into an unexpected hug. For some reason, I had become more of a "hugger" than I had ever been before.

Dad had by then also made his way to the table, carrying an enormous plate, which was piled high with what he had been grilling. "Hey, good timing: Looks like I won't have to reheat, after all," he said, plunking the plate down at the center of the table.

Mom said, "I'll go get Auntie."

"She's here?" I asked, trying to mask my surprise.

"Yes, she's just resting in the spare bedroom. Be right back." She trotted off into the house, while the rest of us sat at the table to wait for the gathering.

I looked at Dad and asked, "What about Aunt Lucille? And the Dodds? Aren't they coming? Shouldn't we wait for them?"

Dad's jovial smile melted, and he donned a more serious countenance. The somber expression on his face worried me. He paused and said, "We weren't sure when to tell you kids, but Myra is ill. I guess you could call it 'gravely' ill. She's in the hospital."

"Since when?" asked Emily.

"She called your mom and me last week. Of course, her sister is looking after her, and Aunt Lucille is just as much their aunt as she is mine, so she decided to stay back there to lend support. There's nothing we can do, really, except hope she pulls through."

Neither Cousin Myra nor her sister—and not Aunt Lucille, for that matter—had ever married, so all they had in the way of support were one another. It made sense, given Myra's health crisis, that they would elect to skip the annual barbecue.

"So, we're going to set that aside for now, at least for today," Dad said. "The six of us are going to celebrate the holiday and enjoy ourselves. We should do this more often. I know that it's partly my fault. Things have been so busy at the shop. Another employee left, and I'm just running ragged."

Mom returned with Auntie. Both were carrying armfuls of various side dishes and beverages. Each seemed to be wincing a bit, as if uncomfortable with the weight their arms bore. In the past, I might have helped Auntie first, but I felt a new-found loyalty toward my true mother, so Mom was the one to whom I went immediately. As if prompted by my offer of assistance, Emily also rose to help Auntie with her load.

Once everything was set, we all returned to our seats at the table, with Mom sitting next to Dad and Auntie directly across from me. Dad started serving the grilled food by taking Mom's plate and using a big spatula to transfer the grub from the serving plate in the center of the table. He looked at her, as if to ask when he should stop; she took the plate at the opportune moment and thanked him. He continued around the table, serving himself last. We each helped ourselves to the side dishes plus a beverage, and then we all dug in.

"Hey, Dad," I said, between bites. "I was thinking… Any chance I could come work down at the shop? You sorta just said that you need the help. Maybe it's time I got involved in the family business."

Dad's quizzical gaze betrayed his astonishment. "I would absolutely love that, Trevor. You didn't seem too interested when I mentioned it a few years ago."

"Yeah, I know. I was confused. I didn't realize then what was important in life. I've had time to think, and I've decided to take up your offer, if you still want to mentor me in the trade."

"What about your career at the bank?" he asked. "I'd need you full-time. There's no going half-way on this. That fiancée of yours—well, really, her father—they're not going to like it if you left your high-powered job at the bank for our little shop. I mean—"

"It's all right, Dad. I've decided to leave the bank anyway. And as for Bianca, I told Mom a little while ago that we broke up for good."

Matt and Emily chimed in to say how sorry they were that things hadn't worked out between Bianca and me. Auntie remained silent. In their collective wisdom, the family came to the consensus that Bianca and I weren't ever a good match and that they had all known that from the beginning. When I asked why no one had told me so, especially before the aborted wedding, my mom observed that there's no accounting for love and that anyone who would interfere with a person's choices in life could only live to regret such meddling.

"Still," Mom said, "your father and I are here in this empty house, and I had so hoped to have a grandchild sooner rather than later. Oh, well. I can't complain, as long as my children are happy; that's all that matters to me."

Emily said, "I was waiting for a good time to break the news… I'm moving in with Cleavon. If I'm reading him right, I think he's almost ready to pop the question."

"Oh, Emily," Mom said. "That's great news. You two make such a lovely couple."

For me, it was more than great news. I had such a nagging guilt that my teenage encounter with Emily might have ruined her when it came to relationships. I had met Cleavon, her boyfriend, a few times and found him to be a genuinely terrific guy: kind, considerate, and emotionally strong—exactly what Emily needed and deserved. If they were cementing their bond with each other, I was not only happy for them too, but I was relieved that she had survived our brief teenage affair intact.

After the merriment and congratulations died down over Emily's news, I turned to Matt and asked, "What about you, little brother? Are you still cynical about relationships? I hope you're inspired by Emily's success in finding love. Don't close your heart to it."

Mom's eyes narrowed as she studied Matt's face, anticipating his response. On her own face was the focused look of worry often associated with motherly concern. Matt must have felt the eyes centered on him, because after a brief pause, he answered, "Don't you guys worry about me. I didn't want to spoil it by telling everyone, but I think, for the first time ever, I might just be, you know, in love." He flashed the goofiest, toothy grin, which made his proclamation all the more innocent and sweetly naive.

He went on to explain that it was one of the high-powered attorneys in the law firm where he worked. He admitted that they had been seeing each other on-the-sly for months and had grown so close that they too had been talking about moving in together. Amid the backslapping, with words of congratulations and encouragement from everyone, my first thoughts turned to Matt's dumpy apartment and what an improvement it would be for him to be able to move out of it. That he would be moving into the loving arms of his lawyer paramour made it seem that much more special.

I couldn't believe that the two siblings I was so worried about had both, somehow simultaneously, been rescued by love, with its power to heal and nurture. The danger of love is when it becomes an obsession, for true love is not about possessing someone or claiming them as one's own; rather, it is discovering the joy one feels in making one's beloved happy and thereby sharing in a happiness one has created together.

I had learned that life was meaningless without love, be it with a mate or from a parent or child: one must remove the doubting "if" that's smack in the middle of the word "Life" and replace it to make it "Love."

Dad steered the table's conversation by turning to Auntie and saying, "You've been awfully quiet there, Alma. How are things going with you?"

Auntie scanned the faces around the table and, with a timid voice, said, "I've thought long and hard about it, and I've decided to retire."

"Weren't you kind of semi-retired already?" Dad asked, although his tone sounded like he intended it as more of a comment than a question.

"Yes, I was down to substituting for therapists who were on sabbaticals or extended leaves-of-absence. I really thought I was helping people. But I've come to realize that psychiatry involves tinkering with things we don't actually understand. I'm not sure we're meant to probe other people's minds."

Dad protested, saying, "I have no doubt you've helped many people in your career, Alma. If you want to walk away from it, more power to you, but you ought to do so without regrets. That's how I plan to retire someday."

Auntie nodded with contentment in response to Dad's encouraging words. I decided to ride the wave of good feeling and discovered that I no longer harbored any ill will toward Auntie or bitterness over what she had done to me. Almost without intending to do so, I spoke my own words of encouragement. "And you'll always be our Auntie."

A pained grin initially came upon Auntie's lips, but it grew into a genuine, beaming smile. "Thank you, Trevor."

I recalled how different the meal had been at the Dawson estate. It was hard to imagine that aloof family displaying much emotion, in the detached setting of their stuffy, museum-like mansion, with servants hovering about as their witnesses—how could they show one another much affection? Yet here, sitting at the picnic table in my folks' back yard, I felt at home, among my beloved family, rooting for Team Wilkins, feeling both supported and supportive, appreciating the company, hearing the occasional, unburdening peals of laughter wash over the party, and most of all, knowing that we all loved one another and cared deeply for the welfare and happiness of each and every person at the table. We were once again, for the first time in a long time, a family, and I could honestly say that family is all that matters in…

THE END

About the Author

Biff Dunnigan was trained to be an attorney but quickly became disillusioned with the American judicial system and chose instead to be a fiction writer.

The author of several short stories, Mr. Dunnigan wrote his debut novel, *The Conceit of Memory*, in the genre of psychological mystery.

He is married and currently lives in Woodland, California.

He welcomes reader feedback. Please visit http://www.PhraseBound.com/authors/BiffDunnigan for more information, as well as how to contact him.